I could die here, Lyon's suddenly thought

It wasn't fear, just an abstract realization. It struck him as almost funny—after all the crap he'd been through in every godforsaken hellhole on earth, he could eat the big one trying to arrest a dope dealer in a little three-bedroom tract house in the middle of L.A.

Something thumped onto the dirty carpet ahead of him. Even before he saw it, Lyon's knew the sound could only mean one thing.

A grenade. Tossed by Buffalo or one of his buddies.

And it was a real one, not a flash-bang.

Mack Bolan's
ABLE TEAM

ABLE TEAM
Fall Back and Kill

Dick Stivers

A GOLD EAGLE BOOK FROM
WORLDWIDE

TORONTO · NEW YORK · LONDON · PARIS
AMSTERDAM · STOCKHOLM · HAMBURG
· ATHENS · MILAN · TOKYO · SYDNEY

First edition April 1986

ISBN 0-373-61223-0

Special thanks and acknowledgment to
Chuck Rogers for his contributions to this work.

Printed in Canada

PROLOGUE

At precisely 10:00 A.M., Eastern Standard Time, a telephone rang at Stony Man Farm. It rang only once before it was answered.

"Brognola here."

The voice on the other end was familiar. "Hal, do you recall our discussion the other day?"

"Yes, sir."

"I've decided to go ahead along the lines we discussed. If the primary approach fails, I want our people to have a secondary option. How was it you put it?"

"If the first approach doesn't work, it's fall back and kill, sir."

"Yes. That's it. Do you think those men you mentioned would be available for this?"

Brognola thought of those men. Able Team. Carl Lyons, "Pol" Blancanales and Gadgets Schwarz. Yeah, they were available. When the request came from the voice on the other end of the phone, *this* voice, they were always available.

"All the way, sir. All the way."

1

Mike Parks was sitting on seven million dollars.

Literally.

The ponderous armored truck pulled away from the First Fidelity Bank Building in downtown Los Angeles. The city street rose in a moderately steep grade, clotted by the noontime traffic. Pedestrians and motorists alike broiled slowly beneath a June smog that pushed down on them like a dirty wool blanket.

In the side-view mirror Parks saw a red Porsche Turbo Carrera swerve out of the center lane and dart ahead to pass the cars in front of it. Its engine made a fine-tuned growl as it leaped forward. The driver had to brake sharply to avoid a collision with the money transport. Angrily he leaned on the horn.

Mike ignored him. The engine and gearbox whined as he slipped the transport into second gear. The massive truck forged ahead.

At the first break in traffic, Mike moved over to the center lane. The driver of the Turbo Carrera seized the opportunity to swerve around the truck on the left. He pulled alongside, still honking rudely. As Mike looked down at him, the driver jabbed his extended middle finger upward, his face contorted by anger.

"Moron!" he shouted.

The driver had curly black hair. His shirt was open to the waist, and several elaborate gold chains were nestled in the man's body hair. He looked about thirty. The sun winked off his bracelets and rings.

"Idiot!" he shouted again, gesticulating wildly.

Mike was unmoved. He had seen the gesture and heard the blare of the horn, but the words were barely audible through the thick bulletproof glass of the armored van.

"Move it!" the driver screamed. "Get that goddamn thing going, you bastard!"

Mike smiled blandly down and waved.

"What is it? Somebody you know?" The question came from Terry Smith, one of the two other men in the van.

"Huh? Oh, that? Nah, just some jerk in a Porsche. Came zooming up on me then got pissed when he had to slow down."

"To hell with him," observed the third man, Frank Adams, from the back of the truck. "As long as he doesn't have a howitzer, what's he going to do? Run us off the road? Spit on us?"

Mike nodded. "I was thinking the same thing. I'll just be cool and irritate him a little." He smiled and waved again at the Porsche's driver.

The horn blared yet again. From the passenger side Terry leaned over to get a look at the driver.

"Nice car," he observed. "I wouldn't mind having one myself."

"Pity I can't just run over the little bastard," Mike responded. "Squash him like a Coors can."

"Against company policy," advised Terry. "Lotta paperwork, too. Besides, at least wait until you're off probation."

"Good point." Mike was only seven months on the job. With a young wife and a child on the way, he needed the paycheck.

The horn sounded again, a long bleat of anger from the sports car.

"Persistent bastard, isn't he? I wonder how he can afford that Porsche," observed Adams from the back.

"Probably a dope dealer. Coke, I'll bet."

SEVERAL CARS BEHIND the armored van and the Porsche was a black-and-white Los Angeles Police Department patrol car. The driver, LAPD Officer Dan Williams, shook his head in disgust.

"Probably a dope dealer. Coke, I'll bet."

"Why do you say that?" Dan's partner was a rookie named Sheila Morrisey. A recent graduate of the Police Academy, Sheila had only been on the streets for three weeks. Dan was her field-training officer.

"Didn't you catch a glimpse of the guy when he passed us? All open-shirted gold-chained curly-headed jerk-offs who drive Porsches are coke dealers. It's one of the great truths of modern society."

Sheila grinned. "Is that a legal principle, Teach?"

He nodded, deadpan. "A natural law, like the law of gravity."

"Who says so?"

"The best cop I ever knew. Guy named Carl Lyons. It was because of him that I joined the department."

"He still on?"

Dan shook his head. "Nope. Left for some Justice Department Strike Force deal. After that he more or less just dropped out of sight." He reached forward and hit the switch for the overhead red-and-blue lights.

"You going to stop this guy?" Sheila's eyes were wide.

"Sure. He's driving a Porsche, isn't he?"

"But we can't do that," she protested. "Just because he's driving a sports car . . ." Then she caught Dan's grin and realized she'd been suckered.

"Relax, partner. I'm not stopping him just because he's a Porsche-driving dope dealer. I'm stopping him because he's driving like an asshole."

"What section of the Vehicle Code is that?"

"I'll think of one."

IN HIS SIDE-VIEW MIRROR, Mike Parks watched in satisfaction as the light bar on the police car came on behind the Porsche. The driver of the sports car was so intent on his ineffectual harangue of the rolling battleship beside him that he didn't see the blinking red-and-blue lights. Finally Mike pointed his finger backward.

"Behind you," he mouthed.

Mike's last sight of the Porsche freeze-framed the driver's furious face. "Who says there's no God?" he said with a grin.

The armored truck turned right onto a side street, and a few blocks later the complexion of the area was completely different. The noon-hour traffic had vanished. So had the crowds.

It was an area of change, the future of the city. New high-rise office buildings were under construction, clawing upward, their beams and girders making rectangular grids in the sky. Deserted buildings, condemned and waiting for the demolition crews, squatted desolately among the job sites.

Yet for all the construction, no workers were visible.

"Man, why is it so deserted?" asked Frank.

"Don't worry about it. Big strike going on. Everybody walked off the job a couple of days ago, that's all," responded Mike.

"Just looks kinda weird, nobody on the streets in the middle of the day."

Mike scanned the streets and nodded. The area did have a surreal atmosphere about it, like the empty streets of a futuristic war zone.

Some three miles ahead lay their destination: the Los Angeles branch of the Federal Reserve Bank.

The Federal Reserve was the "banker's bank." Its job was to collect and disburse operating funds and reserve deposits to all the public banks in the Los Angeles area. Twice weekly, an armored truck like the one they were driving made the route among the member banks. The end of the line was the Reserve.

This was one of those days, a seven-million-dollar day.

The armored truck had a crude, blocky appearance. Its body was a heavy, rectangular box. Even the front end that housed the motor was blunt and stubby. The round heads of bolts that secured the armor plating marched around the body in rows, and the whole affair was painted a dull, unglamorous gray.

Overall, it resembled the mutant offspring of a two-ton delivery truck and a military tank.

A heavy metal post divided the windshield in the middle. On each side of it was a flat slab of thick reinforced bulletproof glass. The single window on each door was made of the same material. Conventional ammunition would spatter or bounce off windows and body alike, and a good many of the so-called armor-piercing rounds would do the same.

It was literally a safe on wheels, cumbersome but impregnable.

So far, anyway. There hadn't been a successful holdup of one of these beasts for the past twelve years.

Video cameras monitored both the driver's area and the cargo hold of the truck. It had taken Mike a few weeks to get used to the lens and the tiny red light that signified it was in operation. One time he had cut out a picture of a nude woman from a skin magazine and taped it so it hung down from the ceiling of the van some six inches in front of the lens.

"Give 'em something different for a change," he had remarked. "This should get their attention."

He wasn't wrong. When the tapes were replayed, the screen showed six hours of knees-to-neck close-up of the model's jutting breasts and fluffy bush.

The boss, a retired captain from the San Diego Police Department, was not amused. The photo came down and stayed down. Mike's probation was extended six months.

Some guys have no sense of humor, he thought.

"What's that?" Terry pointed sharply to a side street twenty yards ahead of them.

"What?"

Mike slowed, instantly wary. A large blue van waited on the side street where it joined the main artery. Then they saw the stylized portrait of a smiling baby on the side of the van. Above it, large pink letters proclaimed Happy Baby Diaper Service.

The driver was an attractive young woman with coppery red hair. She wore a light blue uniform, and she had what looked like a map spread out over the steering wheel.

Mike relaxed. "Looks harmless enough," he said with a grin.

"Doesn't exactly look like the Symbionese Liberation Army," said Terry

"I wonder if she's lost."

"Who knows?" Terry yawned and stretched his legs, fighting the boredom.

"Maybe we ought to stop and see."

"Sure thing, pal. We got seven million dollars in the back, and we're gonna stop to help some lost babe in a tidy-didey truck? That's right out of the rule book, all right." Sarcasm dripped from Terry's voice.

"What's she gonna do? Assault us with a safety pin? Besides, maybe she'll give me a couple of months' free diaper service. I'm gonna be needing it pretty soon."

"Forget it."

As he spoke, Terry leaned forward so his hand was out of the range of the video camera. Then he snapped his fingers sharply and pointed back up at the lens.

Mike got the message. Big Brother was watching. The tape was running. It would ultimately be reviewed by somebody back at the home office—a reminder that boredom was the most insidious enemy of all.

It would be the same Big Brother who hadn't appreciated the "T and A" caper with the nude photo.

"All right." Mike grinned. "I was just testing you."

"Did I pass?" asked Terry, straightening up.

"Yeah, you passed."

At that moment the Happy Baby truck lurched forward. The red-haired girl appeared to fall toward the middle of the truck, as if the sudden movement had caused her to fall off a bucket seat. Mike saw her scramble for the wheel as the blue van rolled into the path of the armored truck.

"Look out!" Terry shouted the warning.

SOP—Standard Operating Procedure—in case anything tried to block the armored car was simple. Keep plowing straight ahead, down-shifting as necessary. Whatever you do, just keep moving. At least, that was the rule for anything smaller than a "semi" or a cement mixer. The momentum and the powerful engine would keep them going through damn near anything.

But that was for somebody attempting to block them off. It didn't apply to what was clearly a routine traffic accident.

Especially from a Happy Baby truck with a girl-next-door redhead driving it.

Mike had a split second's hesitation then hit the brakes. The transport lurched to a stop inches from the blue van.

It was a fatal mistake.

Inside the diaper truck, a hand flipped a switch. Powerful electronic equipment hummed, emitting a broad-band blast of radio waves. It scrambled transmission on all frequencies used by the armored car company—a virtual electronic gag.

The rear door of the Happy Baby van swung sharply open, and six men dropped to the ground.

They wore sleeveless flak jackets and camouflage fatigue pants. Black hoods covered their heads. The first two out carried M-16s, and as Mike watched, they sprinted in opposite directions, scanning the area for danger.

Less than a mile away outside the redevelopment area, thousands of people were going about their noontime business. Here, the only sign of life was a lone wino, staggering toward one of the old condemned buildings, oblivious of what was occurring.

The nearest commando swung his M-16 in that direction. He was a massive brute, Mike saw, maybe six feet, two-forty. Heavy muscles bulged in the man's tattooed biceps as he steadied the weapon.

The short burst slammed the derelict into the graffiti-covered wall of the rat trap. Finding nothing else to shoot, the man waved the others out.

Mike saw two more men sprint toward the rear of the armored van. Each was carrying a dark object, about the size of a small shoebox, and tracking them in the side-view, he saw one disappear around the back of the truck while the other slipped his box just ahead of the rear wheels. Then the man dove out of sight. Only a few seconds had passed since Mike had braked to a halt.

"Haul ass!" screamed Terry. He grabbed for the microphone on the dashboard transmitter. "Code One!" he shouted into the mike. "Attack on Unit Three, corner of Hill and Broadway! Emergency!"

Mike jammed the gearshift into double low and stomped his foot on the accelerator. The engine roared into full power, and the armored car jerked forward at the Happy Baby truck.

At the same moment the muffled blast of twin explosions echoed off the old and new buildings. Mike felt a bone-jarring impact as the truck's undercarriage crashed to the pavement, the rear wheels blown off by the small shape-charges placed there by the two men.

The engine roared, jerked and died as the damaged axles ground into the pavement.

"Home base, do you copy? This is an emergency! Repeat, do you copy?" Terry shouted into the microphone.

A blast of static was the only reply.

The commandos worked with military precision. The last two out of the Happy Baby truck carried a tool the size of a small jackhammer. It was a heavy, diamond-tipped pneumatic drill. A thick cord ran back into the van.

Mike grabbed his .45 while behind him Adams racked a round into the pump shotgun. But they couldn't shoot out any more than the attackers could shoot in.

Their rolling fortress had become a death trap.

Outside, the two men dashed the few steps to the armored transport. They lifted the tool to the window on Terry's side. A sharp, rocky blast cut the air as the gemstone bit chopped through the heavy glass and punched a hole the size of a fist in seconds.

One of the commandos slapped something black into the jagged opening then fell back.

Mike could see the dull black metal of the object.

He knew he was going to die.

With a muffled *whump!* the explosive detonated. Set off in an average-size room, it was guaranteed to stun or kill everybody inside by the concussion.

In the unyielding confines of the armored truck, the results were devastating.

Eardrums burst. The shock waves exploded arteries and scrambled brains from inside the skulls.

The attackers didn't stop to admire their handiwork. The heavy drill was lifted again, and within seconds the doors were open.

To gain access to the rear body and the money, keys had to be inserted simultaneously in the back door and in a special security slot inside the driver's area.

The commandos didn't waste time trying to get the keys from the dead guards. They had their own.

The red-haired girl expertly maneuvered the Happy Baby truck to the rear of the disabled armored truck. The six commandos fell to the task of off-loading seven million dollars into the back of their van.

"EVERY TRAFFIC TICKET you write could be your death warrant."

The ticket given to the driver of the Turbo Carrera had been routine. Officer Dan Williams eased the LAPD black-and-white away from the curb from behind the red Porsche. As he swung back into the traffic, he continued, "Obviously, you can't approach every motorist with your gun out. Your Citizen Complaint File with internal affairs would be even thicker than Carl Lyons's file if you did. But you have to be alert on every one.''

"Alert to what?" Sheila's eyes were solemn as she listened.

"How about this? A couple of years ago two patrol officers in San Diego contacted three juveniles—two guys and a girl—for drinking beer in a park. Sound routine?''

"Sounds routine,'' Sheila agreed.

"Well, turns out one of them had a gun, and both cops were killed.''

"Why, for God's sake? Was he afraid they'd catch him for something else?''

Dan shook his head. "Nobody knows. Guy had a couple of minor warrants out for him, but they were small stuff—misdemeanors—certainly nothing to shoot a cop over.''

"So what's the answer, Teach?''

"Two rules. One, never relax. Ever. That's imperative, whether it's your first or thousand-and-first traffic ticket. There's no such thing as a 'routine' contact until it's over.''

"And the second rule?''

"Watch their hands. Always watch their hands. That's where the weapon will be. That's what will move first if they go for a gun or try to slug you. Got it?''

Sheila grinned. "Got it, Professor.''

"Good. Now let's get out of this traffic and see if we can do some real police work.''

"Such as?''

Dan pointed up ahead. "Not too far off here there's a lot of construction going on. Civic redevelopment. There's a strike on, and we're supposed to be keeping an eye out for possible sabotage. Besides, a lot of drug deals go down in the older buildings.''

Sheila felt a surge of excitement. This was what she had joined the PD for. "Let's go,'' she agreed.

The June heat added to the feeling of desolation in the area. Dan guided the patrol car along, humming softly to himself and wondering idly where Carl Lyons was these days.

Carl Lyons. The "Ironman." His mentor and idol in what seemed a lifetime ago.

Dan was still in high school when his sister and Lyons began dating each other. His sister, Margaret, was in college at the time, working on a master's degree in clinical psychology. Lyons was in his third year with the LAPD, pushing a black-and-white around the city streets.

It was a strange relationship, Dan recalled. Margie was very much "into" understanding people. Sometimes it went so far that people took advantage of her. Lyons, on the other hand, believed in getting the job done—and to hell with the understanding. And yet, despite these differences, there was an attraction between the two that was so strong it was almost tangible.

Dan remembered one occasion when Lyons had been invited to a family barbecue. It had been a hazy day in May, when Dan was a senior in high school. Dan, his dad, Lyons and Margie had been playing pool in the rec room, and a discussion arose over a simple incident in which a belligerent construction foreman had parked his truck in front of a fire lane.

Lyons had located the driver and asked him to move it when he got the chance. The driver, a large burly man with a beer gut and tattoos, ignored him.

That afternoon the truck was still there.

Lyons shrugged and wrote a citation. The foreman tore it up and threw it on the ground. Then he belched in Lyons's face.

Margie, the budding psychologist, shook her head sadly. "The poor man. I wonder what was bothering him to make him do that."

"Who knows?" Lyons chalked his cue stick.

"Usually," Margie continued seriously, "if you don't lose your temper, people will open up to you. You just have to try to communicate with them."

Lyons nodded. "I've found that to be true," he agreed. "It's a matter of relating to them."

Margie looked at him, her eyes shining with pride. "What did you do in this case?"

"I didn't lose my temper, and I communicated with him."

"Were you able to relate to him?"

Lyons lined up his next shot. "Sure was."

"How?"

"In an understanding but firm way I communicated that if he didn't pick up the pieces of the ticket, I was going to kick his ass, feed him the ticket, take him to jail and impound the truck. He related to that, and there was no problem."

Now, years later, Dan smiled to himself as he recalled the incident. Lyons and Margie had been really serious. Marriage seemed a foregone conclusion.

Then, for some reason, things changed. Maybe the differences were too fundamental, after all. And maybe it was something else—Dan never found out, but he had the idea that Lyons had gone through something that brought the gap between his and Margie's outlook into sharp focus. If that were true, it must have been something pretty terrible.

Dan always intended to ask one or the other of them about it. Somehow, though, the time was never right. Then one day the Ironman had come around to see him to say goodbye and to make a prediction of sorts.

"I hope you don't become a cop, but I'm betting you will."

Danny had looked at him in confusion. Lyons had suddenly held out his hand, a grin splitting his face. "And when you do, you'll be a damn good one. Watch your back, Dan, and good luck."

Lyons had been right. He joined the LAPD, following in the Ironman's footsteps, and he never regretted it.

"Looks like a ghost town." Sheila's voice brought him back to the present.

"Strike's making a hell of a difference," he agreed.

Suddenly a bright blue van shot off a side street into their path. Tires screeched as Dan swerved the patrol car sharply to avoid being hit. The van slowed and continued toward the city.

"What the hell?" Dan muttered disgustedly. "Is this the day for every idiot to drive like an asshole?" He swung the car in a U-turn to follow the van, flicking on the light bar as he did.

"Probably just wasn't paying attention," Sheila observed.

Dan nodded. "Yeah, you're probably right. Hard to give a ticket to a Happy Baby truck, anyway. Seems almost un-American. But it wouldn't hurt to give 'em a warning."

The truck yielded and pulled over to the curb. "How about I do the honors?" Sheila suggested.

Dan nodded. "Remember the two rules."

Sheila grinned. "Yeah, and it's not routine until it's over."

"Right."

Dan watched her approach the driver's side of the Happy Baby van. He lit a cigarette and folded his arms, leaning against the patrol unit and gazing over the hot, smoggy landscape.

And forgetting his own rules.

A sharp cry of alarm yanked him back to his senses. Sheila had jumped to one side and was struggling to get her service revolver out of the holster.

She never made it.

An explosion blasted from the van. The young rookie's body suddenly flew backward and landed sprawled on the hard, hot pavement.

In the microsecond after the sound of the blast and before Sheila was thrown backward, Dan heard—or thought he could hear—the impact of the load of buckshot into her body. Part of his mind thought that if it was buckshot she just might live, thanks to the bulletproof Kevlar body-armor vests they both wore. But the force of the impact could be paralyzing, maybe even fatal.

He leaped forward, drawing his revolver. Amazingly, on the pavement, Sheila moved, struggling to bring her weapon up at the van.

Another blast came from the driver's window. Sheila's body flipped over on the pavement.

Dan fired three quick shots at the truck, aiming at the cab just behind the driver's window, praying the bullets would penetrate rather than ricochet.

Suddenly the back of the van opened. Dan whirled to face it.

All he saw were men with guns. Soldiers. Commando types. Camouflage clothing and flak jackets.

Dan emptied his pistol at the men in the van.

He felt a peculiar freedom, as if all the rules were off. He knew he was going to die, and it didn't matter. All that mattered was taking as many of them with him as he could.

With that freedom came a deadly accuracy. All the hangups that normally block a man's reactions had vanished.

The bullets went where he wanted them to, almost as an extension of his thoughts.

Three men died in the van. Head shots. Then the hammer fell on an empty chamber.

Dan leaped forward to the left of the truck, out of the field of fire of the commandos in the back. He swung out the cylinder and dumped the spent shell casings. His left hand found one of the speed-loaders in his belt. It was a round, spoollike device that held six shells in the exact spacing and configuration of the cylinder of his revolver. With practiced efficiency he slipped it into the gun, twisted it free and shut the cylinder.

Even as he did so, he knew it was too late.

A camou-garbed form appeared toward the rear of the van. The commando's arms bulged with muscle. Tattoos ran along the huge biceps and down to the meaty forearms. Dan recognized the man's weapon—an M-16—and knew his body armor would be useless against the hot .223 round.

Both men fired simultaneously.

Dan got off two. The hooded commando fired a full-auto burst.

A paralyzing impact crashed into Dan's chest and his head slammed into the hot pavement. His mind recorded a jumble of images, facts, conclusions—the Happy Baby truck roaring away. The emptiness of the street. The heat from the pavement. Sheila, inches away from him, somehow still alive. And something else, too.

He knew who had shot him. He recognized those arms—the size, even the shape. And most of all the tattoos.

A gaping skull on the left bicep. A tangle of snakes below it. On the right arm, a screaming eagle, diving to attack a dragon.

A word came to his mind, a name. Crank. Crank Krasne. Outlaw biker. Member of the Aryan Brotherhood, a hard-core prison gang that swore to lie or kill for brother members. It had been Dan who arrested him and sent him to prison in the first place.

Behind him, Sheila stirred.

Dan couldn't move his body, but by turning his head he could see her. Her eyelids fluttered open. Her mouth opened and closed and her eyes fixed on him.

Then he heard the words.

"I watched her hands, Teach. Did I do okay?"

Tears welled into his eyes. "You did fine, partner," he croaked. "Just fine."

But she was past hearing him.

2

"Four plates."

Carl Lyons a.k.a. the "Ironman," chalked his hands as he made the announcement.

It was midafternoon at Fisher's Gym in Santa Monica, California. Outside, the June sun heated the city air. For now it was only warm; in a month or so the heat would be at the broiling point. Inside the ancient building old-fashioned fans moved the air around the weights and power racks.

You had to be a hard-core lifter to train at Fisher's. It was just that kind of place.

Large sheets of mirror covered one long wall of the gym. The silver backing was tarnished, and fly specks dotted the glass surface. In front of the mirrors dumbbell racks held matched pairs of iron weights.

The dumbbells ran in increasing weight from left to right. They began with twenty pounds and ended with one-sixtys on the far right end.

"One-sixtys" meant a hundred sixty pounds *each*. The pair weighed three-twenty. Not many men needed that much, though there were a few who did. More of them worked out at Fisher's than at most gyms.

The dumbbells weren't chrome. Dull black was the order of the day.

An array of heavy benches faced the d/b racks and the mirrors. Each had a different angle: a couple flat, one 30 degrees, two more at 45 degrees and one 60 degrees. The variety of inclines could provide a chest workout that made being an oarsman in a Roman galley seem like a picnic.

Behind the incline benches were the power and Olympic lifting equipment—lifting platforms, power racks and bench-press racks. If a member wanted to do dead lifts or clean and jerks, that's where he would go.

Fisher's didn't run tone-up-for-summer specials in the newspaper. It didn't have Jacuzzis, aerobics or racquetball. Its members didn't talk about staying trim; they talked about staying big, or driving for a four-hundred-pound bench press.

It didn't have carpets either, for that matter. The floor was dark cement.

The members were a varied collection of misfits, ranging from ex-cons to cops to beach bums.

"Dinosaurs" would be an accurate term for most of them.

A few months earlier a newspaper reporter came to do a story on Fisher's. It was intended to be part of a series of articles called "Fitness Trends." Each week the story profiled a different gym. The series was supposed to emphasize the social side of working out as well as the exercise part.

Somehow, the reporter had been steered to Fisher's.

She was a pushy type named Pam Martin. She showed up with a tape recorder and camera and set out to put Fisher's on the map. Somebody suggested it might be interesting to interview some of the "dinosaurs" for their perspective on weight lifting and fitness.

"What do you find to be the predominant appeal of Fisher's?" she had asked.

"Huh?" grunted Gred "the Rose" Rosa. He wore navy blue gym trunks, a faded gray tank top with a picture of Mickey Mouse on it, and Adidas with no socks. Pam slid her eyes appraisingly over the slabs of muscle that packed his wide shoulders.

He was loading a fifth pair of 45-pound plates onto the Olympic bar at the dead-lift platform. Five plates on each end brought the weight to 495. The Rose, who had a master's degree in comparative economic theory, considered the day a loss when he did not dead lift six hundred or do a behind-the-neck seated shoulder press with two fifty.

Pam rolled her eyes.

A hunk, but a bit dim, she thought. Undoubtedly a chauvinist, as well. Still, with a back like that, who cares? She simplified the question.

"Why do you like it here?"

"Oh. Lotta iron," he replied.

"No fuck-offs," said somebody else.

"Good atmosphere for lifting," said a third, as if in translation.

"No women," grunted Uhrbach, belching as he spoke.

Uhrbach was about five foot nine and two-thirty. He was broad and squatty, like a refrigerator with muscles. The muscles were covered with the tattoos collected during the several years he had spent behind bars of one sort or another.

It wasn't that Uhrbach didn't like women. In fact, he'd spent four of his formative years in prison for killing a commercial fisherman in a bar fight over a topless dancer. He just had certain ideas about where women should be and what they should be doing.

Such as shaking their bodies onstage at E.J.'s, the topless bar where Uhrbach now worked as a bouncer, instead of running around with cameras and tape recorders, asking questions.

With the intuition that makes a good reporter, Pam was beginning to realize that Fisher's didn't exactly fit the pattern of the gyms she wanted to profile. Still, there was a certain animal magnetism about the place that she found interesting.

An ambience, actually.

She hung around and watched the Rose finish his dead lifts. Her breath caught in her chest as he strained against the six hundred. The Olympic bar flexed from the weight, and the thick muscles of Rosa's traps and shoulders bulged under the strain.

Yes, the place certainly had an atmosphere that was exciting, Pam decided. Before she left, she gave the Rose her phone number and promised Uhrbach she would try out for the amateur night at E.J.'s.

Somehow, though, the article on Fisher's never made it into print.

Next to the lifting platforms stood three bench-press racks. On this June afternoon Carl Lyons was doing bench presses at the center rack with the Rose.

The idea of a bench press is simple. Lie on your back on the bench. Two posts hold the bar a couple of feet above your face. Take the bar off the uprights, lower it to your chest, then push it up again.

Simple. It takes three or four seconds max to do each repetition.

Some guys did six, eight, or anything up to even twelve reps in a single set. Usually, the higher reps were for the bodybuilders, the muscle-beach types who were going for the pump, seeking definition and conditioning. Of course, higher reps meant using less weight.

Lyons took the opposite approach. Heavy weight and low reps.

He did sets of five repetitions at the light weights to warm up. As the weight increased, he dropped to sets of three, then two, then finally one—"heavy singles," he called them.

Every two or three weeks he went for an all-out max on the singles. Each lift was a gut-busting effort.

It was a program well suited to both his mind and his body. At six feet and a shade, the Ironman had a rugged, explosive power that welcomed the challenge of heavy weights. For the past two and a half months he had been lifting hard, and the results showed.

His body weight was up to two-oh-five, and climbing. His strength was at an all-time best.

"How much?" asked the Rose.

"Four plates." In the jargon of power-lifting, that meant four forty-five pound plates on each end of the bar.

"Four-oh-five?"

Lyons nodded. His last rep, at 385, had gone well. This would be a new personal record for him, if he got it.

Things were peaking at an all-around high for the Ironman.

It had been a little more than three months since the last mission. He'd needed some minor surgical repairs for a couple of areas of damage sustained the last time out. After that, he'd spent the time in L.A., divided between his hometown of Montrose, near Glendale, and the beach.

Resting. Healing. Working out.

It was as good a time as any to go for a new max.

Lyons knew something else, too. Not consciously, perhaps, but in his subconscious, in the recesses of his mind.

The vacation was coming to an end.

It was nothing definite. Nobody had said anything about it. There hadn't been any communications from Stony Man

Farm, nothing from Hal Brognola, the "head Fed" and chief of operations at Stony Man. But it was there, nonetheless.

A feeling. A sense of restlessness. The knowledge that while he had needed the break, Lyons wasn't cut out to be a dilettante or a gym bum. It had been fun for a while, but the while was over. And usually when that feeling came around, a mission followed hard on its heels.

Race horses have to run. Warriors have to fight.

Lyons grabbed the block of chalk. Deliberately, purposefully, he rubbed a coat of white onto his palms and the insides of his fingers.

Four plates.

The ponderous weight of four hundred five pounds rested on the posts of the bench-press rack. The spring-steel bar bowed upward slightly in the center from the drag of gravity on the masses of steel at each end. The same masses would soon be pulling the bar down against his chest and crushing the bowed portion of the bar against his ribs.

Lyons glowered at the bar.

It seemed to respond with a sardonic equanimity, a massive and immovable obstacle. "I'll be here when you're rotted and gone to clay," it seemed to say. "Give it your best shot."

Lyons took a deep breath and exhaled sharply. *I'll do better than that,* he promised himself.

Some people believed in relaxing instead of fighting the weight. Experts at martial arts, for instance, advocated that approach. Lyons's friend and Able Team partner, Herman "Gadgets" Schwarz, was one of those. He lifted weights with a metaphysical approach, in a sense becoming "one" with the bar.

Lyons didn't buy that. It wasn't his style. He preferred the frontal attack.

Kick ass or die trying. A berserker. The Ironman.

Four-oh-five waited.

He tossed the chalk back into the tray. Then he gave a quick jerk to his head, both to clear it and to test the tension of his nerves and muscles. Then he strode quickly to the bench, straddled it and lay down on his back.

"Get tough, Ironman!" urged the Rose. "This ain't shit! You can do it!"

Air hissed in a sharp, forced exhalation.

Lyons measured his grip and grabbed the bar. Every nerve was taut and alive. Then, with a quick nod, he signaled for the Rose to help lift the heavy weight free from the rack.

The four plates on each end shifted slightly and clanged as the bar flexed and started downward. Then it was on Lyons's chest. There was a pause, and with an explosive grunt the Ironman drove the weight upward.

The bar slowed as it reached the "sticking point," maybe a foot off his chest.

It was like running into a wall.

This was it. Do or die.

The massive weight hesitated. A high-frequency tremor vibrated in Lyons's triceps as he strained against the weight.

"Push through!" the Rose shouted.

"Drive it, man!" urged Uhrbach from nearby.

The bar didn't move. Then, slowly, inexorably, it broke through, like a ship struggling against a swamping wave.

An inch, then two, then three, and the rest was easy as Lyons locked it out at arm's length over his chest. With a metallic crash, the Rose pulled the bar into the rack.

Four plates was history.

Lyons got to his feet and regarded the bar with a faint smile of satisfaction.

Sure, the weight would be there, enduring and unchanged, long after he was in the ground. But for now, the battle was over. The frontal attack had succeeded. He had won.

Something made Lyons turn around.

Standing in the doorway to Fisher's was a solid, broad-shouldered man with dark skin and black hair that was starting to turn gray. He wore a full but neatly trimmed mustache. His face was strong, the forehead lined, the nose aquiline. He projected a strength that was somehow quite different from that of the weight lifters in Fisher's, though his frame was muscular in its own right.

The stranger's eyes probed the relative gloom of the gym.

Lyons recognized him instantly. "Over here, Pol," he said simply.

The other men in the gym had no way of knowing that, along with Lyons himself, the newcomer was one of the most dangerous men in the world.

Rosario "Politician" Blancanales, one of the fighting men of Able Team, stepped forward. Tension surged through Lyons. Something had to be up.

"Trouble, Ironman." Blancanales's voice was soft and private.

"What is it?"

"There's been a shooting. A couple of cops. Dan Williams."

The name hit Lyons like a fist in the stomach. "Is he dead?"

Blancanales shook his head. "Not yet. He's at the hospital. He wanted to see you."

"Let's go."

That inkling in Lyons's subconscious had finally surfaced. The vacation was over.

3

A black-and-white police car waited at the curb.

The driver, a fit-looking cop in his thirties, wearing the navy blue LAPD uniform, leaned over and opened the passenger door as Lyons approached.

The rear door was locked. Lyons located the heavy wire that protruded from the doorframe inside the front door opening. The lock clicked open. Without a word, Blancanales slid into the back seat as Lyons took the shotgun position in front. The car lurched forward.

"What happened?" inquired Lyons tersely. The crackle of the radio and the unique smell of the patrol car—a mixture of sweat and stale tobacco smoke—brought back familiar memories of his own days on the LAPD.

"Ask him," responded Blancanales, nodding at the officer.

The cop glanced at his passenger. "You Carl Lyons?"

"Yeah."

"I'm Joe Paxton. Central Division. I went through the Academy with Dan. We were roommates for a while after that."

Lyons was aware of Paxton's sideways gaze, a careful sizing up with the peripheral vision.

"So, what happened? Dan get shot?"

Paxton nodded. "Armored car heist. Looks like Dan and a rookie stumbled onto it."

"How bad?"

"Morrisey—the rookie—is dead. Shotgun. Twelve gauge. Looks like she took two. Her vest stopped the first load, but the second one went through."

Lyons let out a long breath. "How about Dan?"

"Critical."

"Still alive?"

"So far."

Lyons remembered another place in another time, and the husky frame of Dan Williams, his girlfriend's kid brother.

Captain of his high-school football team. Fullback. Stocky and tough, but too slow getting into gear to have a future in college or pro ball.

The kid who wanted to be a cop. Lyons had showed him how.

"He get it with a shotgun, too?"

Paxton shook his head. "Negative. A rifle. Looks like a .223."

Nobody had to be the told the vest wouldn't do much good against that kind of firepower.

"How many?"

"Six or seven."

"Jesus." Lyons knew there was no way Dan should be alive.

Blood is incompressible. It doesn't "give" on impact. The hydrostatic pressure would transmit the shock of a hit anywhere to the rest of the body.

Lyons remembered an autopsy he'd attended back when he was on the Organized Crime Strike Force. An FBI agent, a veteran, had taken one round from a .223 in the meat of his thigh. No hits anywhere else.

The cause of death was damage to internal organs over a foot away from the point of impact. "Exsanguination and shock due to rupture, spleen and liver,'' as the pathologist put it.

That guy had been older—fifty—and in nowhere near the shape that Dan was probably in. But six to the chest . . .

Exsanguination.

What a word, Lyons thought.

"Ex" as in without. "Sanguination" from sanguine, meaning blood. Without blood. Loss of blood. A nice, clinical term for spilling your life out on the hot, dirty pavement in a bright red pool that darkens and thickens as the cells die.

If Dan didn't make it, that's probably what the autopsy report would say for him, too.

He wondered if his own would say the same thing, tomorrow or next week or twenty years from now. Whenever and wherever it might be that his own blood ran past the point of no return and he felt himself sucked down into the eternal void of death.

What did it feel like? he wondered.

"Any suspects?" he asked finally.

Paxton shrugged. "Nothing concrete. Dan's gun had two fired in the cylinder, and six dumped empties. A couple of blood spots at the scene don't match up with Dan or the rookie, so it looks like they did some good before . . ." He didn't finish the sentence.

Lyons thought it over. You don't just knock off an armored truck like you do liquor stores or convenience markets. The latter were so easy that cynical cops called them "Stop 'n' Robs," easy targets for every junkie with a gun.

No, this would be different. These guys would be pros, the heist a planned mission.

Well, maybe Lyons could mount a mission of his own.

With a slight yelp from the tires, the police car cut sharply into the emergency entrance to Bay General Hospital.

THE ICU—Intensive Care Unit—was on the fifth floor.

A stocky black man in starched white clothing slid a mechanical buffer back and forth on the linoleum floor of the hallway. The clean, chemical scent of floorwax surrounded them, masking the medical smells. Long fluorescent tubes flooded the hall with white light.

"Why do these halls always seem so long?" muttered Lyons to nobody in particular.

Nobody responded. At last they entered a small room jammed with medical equipment and monitors, in the midst of which lay LAPD Officer Dan Williams.

The medical apparatus was all square cases and precise, even tubes, all very neat and tidy. The human form in the bed somehow looked out of place and irregular in the midst of all the complex devices hooked into it. The initial effect struck Lyons as if a wild animal, a wolf, perhaps, had crawled into a computer and gone to sleep. Or died.

A uniformed cop stood just inside the door. He stiffened then relaxed and nodded as he saw Paxton. On the far side of the bed a woman, an elegant brunette in a beige suit, sat gazing at the still form. She looked up and caught her breath as Lyons, still in his gym shorts and T-shirt, entered the room.

Lyons ignored the woman and strode quickly to the bedside.

Dan lay on his back. His head was tilted back, exposing the heavy sandpaper stubble of beard on his neck. An oxygen mask was positioned over his face. Behind him, a device like a small accordion rose and fell as he breathed. Tubes ran into his arms and legs. Lines peaked and fell on an electronic screen next to the bed, and red electronic digits displayed pulse, blood pressure and breathing rate.

A massive bandage covered the chest. No blood showed, but Lyons could see—or imagined he saw—the darkness of damaged flesh through the white cloth, as if there weren't quite enough layers of gauze to completely hide the color.

Lyons looked at the husky form. A lump formed in his throat. He was no stranger to violent death and had been the cause of a good deal of it himself. But the hospital seemed to focus his awareness of it, somehow making the impending loss seem more acute.

"Dan?" His voice was a hoarse whisper that died in his throat.

"Dan? Can you hear me?"

There was no response. Lyons let his eyes rise to catch the gaze of the woman next to the bed. Her face was solemn and resentful.

Lyons looked back at Dan.

"Dan. Danny boy, can you hear me?"

Long moments passed. Suddenly the eyes flickered open and shut again.

"Come on, Danny. It's me. Ironman."

The eyes flickered open and stayed there, gazing up at the ceiling. Then, slowly, painfully, they focused and tracked over to Lyons's face.

Beneath the foam edges of the oxygen mask the mouth moved in what Lyons knew was a smile.

"Danny, I'm here, man. Margie's here. Don't worry."

There was a faint rustle on the sheets. Lyons looked down and saw the movement. Dan's right hand moved slowly, rotating from where it had been lying palm down, until it rested on its side, the little finger against the sheet.

With agonizing slowness the fingers curled into a fist. Equally slowly, the thumb rose upward. Then the hand flicked in the classic thumb's up gesture, that signal of affirmation that meant anything from "I'm okay" to "give 'em hell."

Lyons was aware that the woman had gotten quickly to her feet and was bending over the bed with him. Eyes watering, he forced a grin and returned the thumb's up gesture.

Dan's eyes held Lyons's for a long moment. Then slowly, almost calmly, they shut again. The fist relaxed back onto the bed.

Lyons realized that for that one moment both of them had known two things. It was a shared understanding, and it was a certainty that both of them had felt it.

Dan Williams was a dead man.

And Lyons had a mission.

Some twenty minutes later the beeps on the monitor turned into a single continuous electronic tone. Alarms went off somewhere in the hospital. Two doctors ran into the room and tried to do something, but there wasn't anything really that could be done, and everyone seemed to know it.

4

"You killed him."

Her voice was accusing and resentful. Lyons ignored her.

"You. You and your macho talk. That's what did it. Not those bullets. All they did was finish the job you started."

"What macho talk?" He didn't really want an answer, but it seemed like he ought to be saying something.

"All that business about being a man and doing what's right and laying it on the line. And for what? For less money than a carpenter gets for pounding nails all day."

"I'm sorry."

"You ought to be. You're the reason he's dead."

When he didn't respond, Margaret continued heatedly.

"He idolized you. Wanted to be like you. And it got him killed." She gave a short, bitter laugh. "What an irony! He wants to be like you and ends up different—you're alive and he's dead. How different can you get?"

Lyons regarded her grimly. She had short brown hair and a face that was slightly too animated to be elegant. She was bright and intelligent. At one time they had talked about a future that would be spent together. Marriage, maybe even kids someday. But now it seemed as if she were a total stranger, somebody he had never even known.

Or worse. Somebody who knew him and despised everything he stood for.

"Look," he said finally. "I'm as sorry as you are. He was a good man, and a brave one. The world has lost a little, and you and I have lost a lot by his death.

"But I didn't kill him. I didn't cause his death. I didn't even make him become a cop."

It was her turn for silence.

"Think about it. You're the psychologist. He became a cop because he wanted to. Because it was right for him. It was his choice, and he made it. Because somebody has to go to bat for the underdogs, the victims, the ones who can't fend for themselves."

"And so you and all those bullyboys do it," she said derisively. " 'The magnificent seven' rides again. Only it'll be six now, won't it?"

For a moment Lyons felt an irrational urge to backhand her. But that wasn't right, either. She was hurting, and he was a handy target for the grief that poisoned her.

How could he ever explain it? It was the kind of thing that if you didn't already know, you probably weren't capable of knowing.

The hell of it was that part of what she said was right on target. It *was* a question of good and evil and doing what had to be done, because you were the guy who could do it.

Lyons had known this as a young cop. Danny Williams had known it.

He turned toward her and gripped her by the shoulders, turning her to face him. She looked away.

"Listen, Marge," he said softly. "Hear me out. Not for my sake, but for Danny's."

"How does this help Danny now?" Tears glistened on her cheeks.

"By giving him the credit he's entitled to. By helping you remember him for what he was, rather than as if he was some witless kid who died for nothing, playing some silly game."

She didn't respond.

"Your brother didn't do it just for a job. He didn't do it for fun. He did it because there are strong ones and weak ones out there. A lot of the weak ones are good people. They're just poor. But they feel things just like you and me. Some of the strong ones are vultures. Sharks. They prey on the weaker ones. Somebody has to stop it."

Margaret looked into his eyes for the first time. "Why did it have to be Danny? Why does it have to be...?"

She let the sentence trail off. Lyons wondered if she had been about to say "you," in reference to himself. Or was that just wishful thinking?

"Because he *could*," Lyons responded gently. "It's as simple as that. You've got to be just as strong as the sharks to jump into the water with them. Dan had what it takes and thought he should use it."

"It seems like such a waste. So useless." Her voice was a whisper.

Lyons shook his head. "It isn't. Guys like Dan Williams and me, and some others I could name—we're good at the things that are necessary to protect the weak ones."

"Like killing people?" The bite was back in her voice.

"Sometimes."

She was silent for several moments. When she spoke again, her voice was tired.

"I just don't know. I can't believe that force is the answer. There's got to be a better way. Maybe if you weren't so quick to use force, maybe if you tried another approach..."

"Maybe," Lyons agreed. "But until somebody finds another way, we're left with force. Whether or not you agree with it, at least accept that it's a valid theory. That way,

Danny died doing something he believed in, and for a reason he thought was good. It'll make his death seem less of a waste."

"Is that how you rationalize it?"

"Yes," he replied simply. There was nothing more to say. "Look. Where are you parked? I'll walk you to your car."

She started to object then thought better of it. "Basement. Lower level three."

The elevator let them out onto a concrete apron. The parking garage was gloomy and dark, even though it was still light outside. Only a handful of cars remained.

"Which one's yours?"

"Over there." She pointed. "The BMW."

It was parked on the oil-stained concrete near the far wall, diagonally across from the elevator. The overhead lights in that area had been broken, leaving it even darker than the rest of the garage. Overflowing with boxes, a dumpster had been overturned in front of the car, blocking it in.

"Good choice," Lyons said sarcastically.

"The car?"

"No. The parking space."

"It was the only one available when I got here."

He took her by the arm. "Come on. I'll walk you over there."

"Still the knight in shining armor," she commented, but she smiled as she said it.

Margaret's heels echoed in the garage as they crossed to the car.

Suddenly Lyons gripped her forearm.

"Hold it!"

As if by way of answer, something moved behind the car. A gang of Mexican youths stepped out from the shadows.

Margaret stiffened. A sharp intake of breath hissed between her teeth.

There were five of them. Lyons checked them over with a practiced eye.

Gang members. Marauders. Hoods.

Their ages: late teens to early twenties. Three of them looked pretty buffed out; the other two were more thin than strong. Black pants, white socks on all five. Long-sleeved Pendleton-style shirts with red-and-black checks, shirttail out rather than tucked in. Sleeves worn down, probably to hide the track marks from street heroin shot into veins picked open with straight pins. Red bandannas, folded to make a two-inch red band around the forehead.

Two of them had teardrops tattooed beneath the corner of their eyes.

Originally, the teardrop meant the man who wore it had been to prison or had killed somebody. Lyons knew, however, that a lot of youths wore them these days without having done either.

"Hey, pretty lady. We been waitin' for you."

The speaker was one of the muscular ones. His voice was hoarse, guttural. Deep pockmarks pitted his gaunt face, and a long dark scar ran down one cheek. There were two teardrops beneath his left eye. From the looks of him, he might have earned them the hard way.

A familiar anger rose in Lyons.

"Take a hike, asshole!" he snapped.

The one that had spoken laughed. His teeth looked as bad as the rest of his face. His eyes glittered in the dim yellow light.

"Hey, man, no. I mean, no way, man. We been waiting for this pretty lady. We gonna have some fun. You like that, *chica*?"

"Look," said Lyons. "I'm in no mood for this shit. Haul ass before I lose my temper!"

There was a sharp click as a blade leaped out in the hand of the leader. From nowhere, knives or clubs appeared in the hands of the others.

Margaret gave a sharp gasp of fear. The leader laughed.

"You afraid, pretty lady? Maybe we let your boyfriend watch. You like that?" He turned and struck a savage blow to Margie's car with the pipe he held in his hand. The crash reverberated off the walls. The fender showed an ugly crease where the blow had struck.

Lyons began to back up, keeping Margaret behind him.

The leader made a sharp gesture with his head. His companions began to walk slowly to either side, spreading out, making a semicircle in front of their intended victims.

Lyons turned his head to one side and spoke softly out of the side of his mouth. "Well, what do you think? Is this a case for force, or shall I try another approach?"

Anger overcame fear. "You bastard!" she muttered.

"That I am," he said grimly. He stopped backing up, then took a step forward, toward the gangsters.

They stopped.

The rugged blond man with the build of a weight lifter was not playing the game right. When the *chollo locos* pulled knives and bats, victims were supposed to cave in. This one wasn't going along with the program.

"You a cop?" the leader demanded.

Lyons shook his head. "Nope," he replied simply.

The thug considered it for a moment. Maybe the blond man was an ex-con. Most men in prison lifted weights. Moreover, in the brutal society of convicts, almost all inmates became one of two things—takers or givers. The strong or the weak. Yes, that might account for both the man's build and his attitude.

"You been to the joint, man?"

"Nope."

The leader made an angry slash of the air with his blade. "Then what the fuck's wrong with you, anyway?"

Like the rest of his Able Team partners, Lyons had received martial arts training. Still, he wasn't a skilled technician in unarmed combat the way Blancanales was. Instead, he combined a few basic karate skills with another fighting tactic.

Instant fury.

Plain, mad-dog anger. Zero to sixty in a flash. Animal meanness. A wild man's rage when he needed it. And that, added to even rudimentary martial arts training, made him nearly unstoppable. The combination had served him well from the streets of L.A. to the jungles of Central America.

"Well?" the *chollo* demanded.

Lyons smiled. It was a thin and not very pleasant smile. When he spoke, his voice was deliberately soft and low.

"Fuck you, punk."

The leader jerked as if he'd been jolted by electricity. His blazing eyes narrowed to slits. Then his lips parted in a maniacal grin. Turning to his companions, he jerked his head in the direction of the blond man. The semicircle advanced. The dim light winked off long, sharp blades.

Lyons got set up, ready for action. He felt strong, alive. His gym clothes and nylon shoes were free and unconfining. He sensed Margaret behind him, backing slowly away.

As they moved forward, he exploded into action.

His right foot flashed forward like a bullwhip. Propelled by the length of his leg, it snapped into the groin of the closest *vato*.

Instant paralyzing pain hit the gangster. It shocked his system from below like an earthquake. He folded and fell, retching on the dirty cement.

Lyons used the forward motion of his body as the source of power for his next move. Turning to his left, he brought

a sharp right-handed blow into the face of one of the attackers.

Cartilage popped and a fan-shaped spray of blood shot
from the man's nose.

In the same movement Lyons reversed himself and swung
back to his right side. This time it was the back of his fist
that took out one of the converging punks. It hit with a
bone-on-bone smack against the side of the man's jaw.

Lyons felt the force of the impact clear up to his shoulder.

The punk felt it clear down his spine. He dropped as if he
had been poleaxed.

Lyons spun away and set up again. The blood roared in
his ears as he crouched and circled the two remaining hoods.

The three who were down weren't getting up. One moaned
and clutched his groin. The sour smell of vomit mingled
with the petroleum smells of gas, oil and tire rubber. The
second lay on his back, head tilted back, both hands
clamped on his shattered face. The third lay slackly on the
floor.

For an instant the remaining combatants gazed at each
other. Then Lyons attacked.

He feinted at the nearer one, a thin youth with the dull
glazed eyes of a junkie. The frightened response told him
that one was no threat.

The other one was. He held a piece of blunt gray pipe
some fourteen inches long. The end was capped off, and a
bent nail protruded from it. Lyons guessed the end of the
pipe was weighted, filled with cement, probably. The *chollo*
held it out to one side and in front. He alternated flicking it
from side to side and making short, jabbing motions.

Lyons respected the movements. They were much more
versatile and deadly than simply clubbing down from over

the head. More than that, it showed the man might know what he was doing.

Crouching, Lyons moved forward. Catlike, he swiped out a long arm at the *vato's* legs, like a wrestler going for a takedown.

The man dodged backward, out of range.

Just as quickly, Lyons advanced. Again he swiped a hand out for the man's leg.

The *chollo loco* didn't need another opportunity. As Lyons went in low, the gangster raised the short heavy pipe high and smashed it down from above.

It was what the Ironman had invited him to do.

Instantly, Lyons's hands shot up and grabbed the descending arm. He pivoted away and executed a hip throw, using the man's arm as a lever to heave the body up and over his own back.

In the gym you let go of the arm as the man comes over your back.

On the streets you don't. Lyons held on to the wrist and whipped the punk's body headfirst onto the cement.

The man's head broke open with a sound like a not quite ripe watermelon dropped onto concrete from a stepladder.

The last of the would-be predators turned and fled.

Lyons watched his retreat. What the hell, let him go, he thought. Then he remembered what this was supposed to be—five armed marauders attacking a lone woman, using her, discarding her, maybe killing her.

It wasn't due to any decent impulse that the punk was leaving. He just got scared when the odds changed from five on one to three on one, then to one on one.

To hell with him. He shouldn't get any credit for that.

Lyons sprinted across the underground garage. His gym shoes gripped the pavement and he flew after the retreating gangster. From behind him, he heard the urgent cry from Margie.

"Carl, no!"

The Ironman ignored it. He closed the gap as though the punk was standing still. The man turned at the last minute, in time for Lyons to club him at the base of the neck. Lyons swung the heel of his hand in a single powerful swipe.

The man flew headfirst, landed on his stomach and skidded into a concrete beam.

Lyons slowed to a trot and jogged in a circle back to where Margaret stood. One look told him she would never understand. But it didn't matter. Maybe it was good the world had people like that.

People for whom guys like he and Danny Williams could fight. And when the time was right, die for.

That was what it was all about. If the tame and gentle Margie Williamses of the world looked on him as a dinosaur, so be it.

These *vatos* had opened the door. All he had done was walk through it. And, in so doing, he had balanced the books a little. Nothing wrong with that.

But there was another set of books that had become seriously out of balance. Danny Williams was gone, along with a rookie named Morrisey, whose first name he didn't even know. That made a heavy deficit on one side of the ledger.

Rest in peace, Danny, he thought. I'll make sure the bill goes out on that account.

And I'll collect it.

Personally.

5

"Face it, Ironman, she just doesn't understand."

The Federal Building in downtown Los Angeles loomed before them. Lyons digested Blancanales's words as he maneuvered his rented sedan through a narrow concrete channel that led to the underground parking area.

"No, but you didn't help much."

Blancanales feigned innocence. "What do you mean?"

"You know damn well what I mean."

Lyons had been debating whether to call the cops in the aftermath of the attack in the hospital parking garage. At the same time, he had been trying to ignore Margaret's vocal criticisms of his actions.

Her about-face had been awe-inspiring.

The crisis behind her, Margaret had put aside how close she had come to being gang raped and probably murdered, as well. Instead, she had turned her attention to critiquing Lyons's reaction to the attack.

She hadn't minded that he took out the first three gang members. She was even okay about the fourth, though it seemed a little drastic to break the punk's head open on the concrete. But what really upset her was Lyons's pursuit of the fifth one as he fled the scene.

"Why, Carl? Couldn't you understand it was only peer pressure that made him go along with the others? Couldn't you see there was no need to go after him?"

Lyons looked at her in amazement. He felt as if he were in some kind of reality warp, a nonsensical fifth dimension. It made about as much sense as saying the Russians really meant to go along with arms limitation or that the California Supreme Court cared about the rights of anybody else except the criminals.

Had she changed? Lyons knew she was always more liberal, not to say open-minded, than he. But he didn't remember it being chronic, not like this. Maybe it was one of those things where the words are not really what's being communicated, but were actually a vehicle to engage in hostilities born of some other basis.

"You heard me. That boy was no threat after you had subdued his associates. But you couldn't just let him go, could you? Oh, no, not you. You had to run him down and beat him up, too."

Enough was enough.

"No, I didn't *have* to run him down and beat him up. I did it because I wanted to."

"I can't believe you," she retorted, her voice a mixture of disgust and indignation.

At that moment the elevator doors had opened and Blancanales stepped out. He had stayed behind to talk to the doctors, as well as to give Lyons and Margaret some privacy. When he caught sight of the battlefield, he sprinted across the garage to where they were standing.

"Everything okay?" he asked.

Lyons nodded. "Just after the nick of time, as usual," he observed.

Blancanales surveyed the moaning bodies. "Sorry. I didn't realize you intended to wipe out the entire gang population of L.A. this afternoon."

"Give him the chance, and he'll try it," interjected Margie bitterly.

"He's always been that way," agreed Blancanales, his voice sympathetic.

"I was trying to tell him that automatic brute force isn't the only answer."

Pol shook his head sadly. "It's the standard primitive response for some people. Unfortunately, in the long run it just lowers man to the level of animals."

"Do you really believe that?"

He nodded. At this show of support, Margaret looked triumphantly at Lyons. When her head was turned, Blancanales rolled his eyes and stroked his forehead as though he had a headache. When she turned back, however, his expression was serious.

"I'm glad that at least *somebody* understands. Fighting and bloodshed never really solved anything."

"Absolutely. Violence begets violence. Besides, this shows he's not only a complete barbarian and savage, but he's totally self-centered and selfish, as well."

Margaret frowned. Insensitive, she understood. But the rest? "Why selfish?" she inquired.

"I was only a minute or two behind you guys. He knew that. But did he wait? Did he think to share any of this with his best friend? Hell, no, he didn't! He hogged all the fun for himself!"

Lyons remembered the screech of tires as Margaret left. If he hadn't jumped to one side, the BMW would have clipped him as it went by. He shook his head.

"Well, one thing's for sure."

"What's that?"

"Any chance I might have had of patching things up is history now."

Blancanales considered the comment. "Maybe," he agreed. "And maybe not. Women are a lot like the income-tax laws. Incomprehensible. Impossible to understand. They give at one point and take back at the next. And most of all, they're inconsistent. She could be calling you up by tomorrow.''

"I doubt it. Anyway," he said, changing the subject, "did the doctors say anything?"

"No, amigo. Nothing that we didn't know, anyway."

"Tell me."

Pol shrugged. "He was one very tough *hombre*. Multiple high-velocity projectiles to the chest. It's amazing he hung on as long as he did."

"Was he able to describe who did it?"

Blancanales shook his head. "He wasn't in any shape to talk to the medical people, though he did regain consciousness for a few minutes after he was stabilized. The doctor thinks he may have said something to the sister, but he doesn't know what. End of report."

Lyons thought it over. "It's not much, is it?"

"It never is."

A UNIFORMED SECURITY GUARD stopped them at the entrance to the underground federal parking area. Lyons identified himself. The guard consulted a computerized list of names. He went through it twice without success.

"You're not cleared. You can't park in here."

"I have an appointment with Roger Haines, FBI, Special Agent-in-Charge."

"Maybe you do. But this is a secured area, and unless you're cleared, you'll have to park on the street." The tone of voice was surly.

"Look," Lyons said tightly, "do yourself a favor. Get on the phone and call Haines's office. Ask if there's clearance for Stony Man."

"Why should I?"

"What kind of hospitalization plan does your company provide?" As he spoke, Lyons's jaw jutted dangerously.

The guard gazed at him for a long moment. Finally he sauntered over to the telephone. He dialed, spoke, and listened. When he returned, his attitude had undergone a radical transformation.

"Go right in, Mr. Lyons. Sorry for the inconvenience. Mr. Haines is expecting you. Turn left and park at the end, in the stalls marked FBI."

Actually, there was no appointment with Roger Haines. The SAC wasn't even available, in fact. But there had been a call from FBI headquarters in Washington, D.C., and the orders were very clear.

A couple of guys named Lyons and Blancanales would be showing up. They were involved in an ultrasensitive program, code name Stony Man, no further details, need-to-know only. The SAC had also been told to provide any assistance requested, and specifically to have a secure telephone line available for them.

The orders brought action. Instant action. Ten minutes later, Lyons and Blancanales were sitting in a featureless government room, getting ready to hook up with the head Fed, Hal Brognola.

The room was U.S. Government issue all the way. Beige metal walls, sturdy brown nylon carpet, a heavy metal door painted a dark brown. There was a gray steel table with a Formica top, two battered chairs and a wastebasket.

"Class accommodations," Blancanales observed.

"Do you care?"

"No. Usually the FBI is a bit more plush, that's all."

Lyons grinned. "That's the supervisors' offices you're thinking about. This is a workroom, man."

"Sorry. I forgot."

Two standard black telephones rested on the table. Lyons picked one up and went through the drill to place a secure call to the other side of the country. Blancanales listened in on the other.

Stony Man Farm.

The nerve center of Mack Bolan's New War. A quarter section—one hundred sixty acres—in the Blue Ridge Mountains, a short helicopter-jump from the White House and the Pentagon.

Bolan lived there—they all lived there, if they lived anywhere.

In a very real sense, Bolan and his teams of specialists lived nowhere, yet lived everywhere. It was part of being somebody whose life was to fight anywhere in the world on a moment's notice.

It goes with the territory.

Along one wall of the War Room in the basement of the main house at Stony Man Farm was a huge map of the world. Borrowing an old joke from his days on the LAPD, and later on the Federal Strike Force, Carl Lyons had inked a neatly printed label onto a three-by-five index card. Then he had stood on a chair and taped it over the map.

It was an ironic commentary of the job he and the others had signed on to do.

It contained four words.

Able Team Beat Map.

Lyons had done that right after South America. It had been an all-too-brief hiatus, barely a breather. Then things had gone to hell in Egypt, and Able Team found themselves en route on Code Three, as Lyons called it—red lights and sirens. Lyons had printed out the makeshift label and stuck it in place before they left.

What was significant today was that Hal Brognola would be standing by for the call to come through.

Brognola, known with affection and respect as the head Fed of the Stony Man group, had spent his adult life in the secret world of covert operations. These days he carried the title of director of the Sensitive Operations group. More importantly, he was Stony Man's liaison with other related groups of the executive branch, from the CIA to the White House. It was a delicate and difficult job, especially since the Stony Man operation wasn't supposed to exist.

Like any good control, Brognola was there when he was needed. Today was no exception.

"Evening, Boss," said Lyons.

"Carl, my boy! So good of you to call!" Brognola's genial voice boomed over the line from a continent away. "Hang on a sec while I check the line."

Lyons heard the hard plastic click of buttons being pushed. He could visualize Brognola with the inevitable cigar clamped between his teeth. Right now he would be energetically jabbing at a computer keyboard adjacent to the phone. In a moment the voice came back on.

"Clear," Brognola confirmed. "Report."

"Five nothing, bottom of the first."

The meaning wasn't lost on Brognola. "Five? The second officer, died, too? The one you knew?"

"Affirmative." Lyons felt his voice strangely close to being shaky.

Brognola sighed. When he spoke again, his voice sounded tired, a little worn, perhaps. "I'm sorry."

"Yeah. Me, too. Question."

"Shoot."

"Who did it?"

There was a pause. Brognola's reply was cautious. "What makes you think I know, Carl?"

"I can add two and two, for God's sake!" Lyons snapped. "You didn't send Pol out just to help me out because the kid brother of an old girlfriend got shot. It's not your style. Besides, there wouldn't have been time."

"Go on," said Brognola quietly.

"The only way the timing would work is that you sent Pol out to find me. That means you've got a job lined up. Then suddenly three armed guards and two cops get blown away in a paramilitary assault on an armored car. You know what I think?"

"What?"

"Coincidences happen, but not in this business. Not often, anyway. Certainly not like this. This has 'pro' written all over it. I think the only coincidence was that I happened to know one of the guys who bought the farm."

There was a silence at the other end of the line. Then the Stony Man director spoke, his voice resigned. "You're right. Guilty as charged. Like they say, you may be crazy, but you ain't stupid."

"So, what's going on?"

"There's a group we've been asked to look into out there. It's a domestic terrorist outfit, and a damned scary one. We had information from a closely placed, generally reliable source that something heavy was coming down."

"Details?"

"Only a few. The source said the group was getting ready to make a major weapons acquisition. Mainly infantry weapons. Enough to equip a small army, if the information is correct."

Lyons nodded, forgetting that Brognola couldn't see him. "Well, that fits. Seven million dollars will buy a lot of guns."

"We didn't know it was going to be this, of course. Like I said, details were scarce. The source didn't specify either a robbery or a time frame."

"So who are these guys?"

"Officially—and this is classified—they're known as Group 504. Unofficially, they call themselves the White Knights."

Lyons gave a snort of laughter.

"What's so funny?" Brognola asked sharply.

"The White Knights, for God's sake! Why not Sister Sue's Sewing Circle? How can you take a bunch of dip-shits that call themselves the White Knights seriously?"

"Why don't you ask Danny Williams?" Brognola's voice was cold.

Lyons's jaw tightened in sudden fury. But the Chief was right, of course. Lyons's anger was directed at himself, not Brognola. "Sorry," he said tersely. "Go on."

"You familiar with the ATO, Ironman?"

"That directory of all the terrorist groups? Yeah, I think so."

"ATO stands for Analysis of Terrorist Organizations. It's put out by a joint task force of the CIA and the FBI. It contains every bit of reasonably accurate data on all the main terrorist groups in the world."

"Do you have access to one?"

"Yes. At least, insofar as it deals with Group 504. It divides the terrorist organizations into five classifications, with Class 5 being the worst. The White Knights are the fourth group listed in Class 5. That's where they get the 'Group 504' label."

"What's all that mean in plain English?"

"It means they are some real bad guys."

"So what do you know about them?"

"Classic terrorism coupled with white supremacy. They make the Ku Klux Klan look like a bunch of left-wing liberals. They are closely allied to outlaw motorcycle gangs along the lines of the Hell's Angels, and to prison gangs such as the Aryan Brotherhood. Their ultimate goal is to overthrow the government and establish their own.''

"That's a tall order.''

"Yes, it is. But they believe they can do it. And it doesn't stop them from doing a lot of damage and killing a lot of people along the way.''

Lyons thought about Danny Williams, and how his stocky frame had seemed to dwindle and subside—to flatten out somehow—when the life had left his body. A slow, cold rage began to come over him.

"And these are the ones responsible for the armored car heist today?''

"That's been confirmed.''

"And they're the ones you were going to have us go after?''

"Yes.''

Lyons looked at Blancanales, who was listening on the other phone. "It'll be a pleasure.''

"Maybe,'' Brognola said. "And maybe not. There's one hitch.''

"What's that?''

"This isn't your usual 'kill 'em all and sort the bodies out later' kind of a caper. I want you to get them legally.''

"Legally?'' Shock and dismay showed in Lyons's voice.

"Legally?'' Blancanales echoed.

"That's right. On this mission you'll have to be thinking arrest and conviction, not search and destroy.''

"You mean working with some tight-ass Ivy League Justice Department lawyer in a three-piece suit and a hundred reasons for not doing what has to be done?''

"Not exactly. This guy isn't like that.''

"They all are,'' Lyons said disgustedly.

"Not this one. He's one of us. You know him from that cocaine caper a while back." Brognola paused, then continued. "His name is Mike Chandler."

Brognola's announcement came as a shock in more ways than one.

For one thing, Able Team wasn't designed to "do it legally," in the sense of seeking an arrest and conviction. "Body count" didn't mean "number arrested." The team itself—the entire Stony Man operation, in fact—had been created to fill the growing void between where the law ended and justice began.

As Mack Bolan himself once put it, "There's too damn little justice in the Justice Department these days."

Moreover, it just wasn't their style. Leave the finer points of arrest and conviction to the lawyers and judges. And the cops, poor bastards, who had to struggle with the technicalities created by ivory-tower liberals with floppy briefcases, whose closest exposure to crime was picking up the paychecks they didn't earn.

Lyons knew. He'd been a cop once and had struggled with the legal technicalities designed to free criminals. But those days were gone. Now things were different. "At least we don't have to advise the dirt-bags of their constitutional rights in the middle of a firefight," he once remarked.

In other words, Able Team wouldn't be there in the first place if the legal system hadn't already broken down.

The other shock, albeit a pleasant one, was the news they'd be working with Mike Chandler.

Lyons had often wondered what had become of Mike. They had met a few missions back, at the outset of what was to become a bloody war with major Colombian cocaine traffickers.

At the time Chandler had been with the D.A.'s office in San Diego. Tall and rangy, a Vietnam veteran and a former

Golden Gloves boxer, Chandler had shown the fighting spirit that made him a winner in and out of court. But the law had failed, and the blood of innocents had been the price of the failure.

It was time for justice. Based on a recommendation by Mack Bolan, Able Team had taken a chance on Chandler.

He hadn't let them down. Together they had pursued the forces of Enrique Raul Castro into the steaming jungles of Colombia. Together they had seen Castro pay the final price for his cruelty.

Chandler was a man, in a world where there weren't many men.

Brognola's instructions were clear. "Chandler's working with a Federal Strike Force these days. Their headquarters are in L.A. in the old Federal Building Annex. Be there at 0800 hours tomorrow."

With the instructions came a warning. It was directed at Lyons. There was no mistaking that Brognola meant it.

"There's one more thing, Ironman."

"What?"

"This is a mission, not a vendetta. You get my drift?"

Lyons did, but a perverse streak refused to acknowledge it. "Spell it out, Boss."

"All right. I will. We're not in the revenge business. The purpose of this assignment is not to give you a vehicle to settle any scores. Vendettas are personal, and missions are bigger than that. Understand?"

Lyons thought of his silent promise to the dead cop he'd once known. "I understand. In theory I agree. But theory sometimes looks pretty limp next to reality."

"If you can't handle it, I'll pull you out. If you jeopardize the mission for your own ego, I'll pull you out. This job means more than any one man's feelings, and that includes yours. I mean that a hundred percent.'' Brognola's voice was tight.

"That's plain enough, I guess. Question, though.''

"Sure.''

"Why?''

Brognola paused. "Why what?''

"Why are we doing it this way? Why are we doing it at all? Hell, if you want it done the Supreme Court way, use the FBI. Hell, we don't even have law-enforcement powers.''

There was a silence. When Brognola spoke, his voice had lost its hard edge.

"That's a fair question, I guess. You're right. I know it isn't our style. But we're doing it this way because we've been asked to.''

"I don't understand.''

"Let me put it this way. It's something that we ought to be doing. The target is right up our alley. It's just the methods that aren't.''

"Any chance we can change the methods?''

"Don't worry. I'm working on it. In the meantime, you've got to be doing it, as you put it, the Supreme Court way. And this has another advantage, as well.''

"What's that?''

"You're forgetting that we don't even know who is the big cheese behind the White Knights. The Strike Force is working on that. You'll be in a position to help them, and, of course, then you'll know yourselves. Maybe by then we'll have a different set of rules.''

Lyons began to see the big picture through the mists. Able Team had to operate under certain parameters set by Brognola and Stony Man. Those two, in turn, were subject to pressures and guidelines created by political or other strategic considerations.

Also, knowing Brognola, if this were how it had to be, Hal wasn't any more pleased about it than they were. Which meant he would be trying his damnedest to get the rules changed.

After a moment Brognola spoke again. His voice had that speculative quality that said "read between the lines, this is bureaucratic double-talk."

"Of course, you're not expected to go into this thing naked. You're still entitled to defend yourselves, and if a life gets lost here and there in the course of doing it legally, there's nothing wrong with that."

"I see," Lyons responded, his voice expressionless.

"Moreover, if it even happens that a little personal satisfaction is achieved along the way, that's perfectly proper, too. Especially if it is merely incidental to achieving the mission."

Lyons grinned into the phone. What a guy, he thought. No wonder Bolan has him directing Stony Man operations. "I agree that it's important to obtain fulfillment from doing one's job. Strictly within the goals of the mission, I mean."

"Call it one of the perks of the business," Brognola agreed. "Just don't do anything that will come back to burn me. Got it?"

Lyons got it. From across the table, Blancanales winked at him.

"Loud and clear, Boss. Loud and clear."

"Stony Man out."

6

Strike Force Prosecutor Mike Chandler didn't expect what walked through the door the next morning.

The instructions were clear enough. Chandler's team had located a clandestine "safehouse" used by associates of Group 504, a.k.a. the White Knights. The suspected occupants of the safehouse were weapons freaks, and good for at least three killings, besides.

That didn't count the armored-car hijacking yesterday. Though he hadn't heard officially, Chandler was sure that the same people were involved in it.

It looked like the break they'd been waiting for, and it was long overdue. If they hit big, the house could lead them to the inner circle of the White Knights. If they blew it, it would be back to square one. Because of that, the Justice Department was sending more manpower.

They didn't give him any names. The orders just said one of his men should pick them up at the old Federal Building Annex in L.A. and escort them to the Strike Force headquarters.

Three men, he was told. All had the necessary clearances.

Were they experienced, he had asked. He couldn't be saddled with rookies at this stage of the case.

Don't worry about it, they told him.

Well, he could use them. It would be a one-third increase in his manpower. With the warrant coming up, Chandler needed bodies, preferably trained bodies.

Chandler's investigation was part of a much larger, nationwide effort run by the U.S. Justice Department. Designed by the President to combat both domestic and transnational terrorism, the program combined personnel and resources from a variety of state and federal law enforcement agencies.

The theory was to create a number of separate strike force teams, each designed to target a specific terrorist group. In law enforcement jargon, it was called "pro-active." As Chandler sometimes explained it, "we investigate criminals, not crimes."

His Strike Force team had nine men in addition to himself. The nine were cops of one sort or another. All had been sworn in as special federal agents. Two were investigators from the California Department of Justice. One was a deputy sheriff with the L.A. Sheriff's Office Special Crimes Bureau, and one was from the beleaguered LAPD Criminal Intelligence Unit. The others were full-time Feds, two FBI agents, two deputies of the United States Marshal, and one man from the CIA.

Nine agents and one prosecutor. When the cases went to court, it would probably have to be the other way around.

Chandler himself had been recruited from the D.A.'s office to head the team. He called the shots, got the warrants and tried to hold the nine diverse egos together despite the inevitable interagency rivalries.

Group 504 was Chandler's assignment.

Locate them. Follow them. Find out what crimes they're committing and get them for it. Whether it's narcotics, illegal weapons, murder or just playing their stereos too loud;

the crimes didn't matter. Just make sure it was something that would stand up in court.

It was a tall order. Right now they were still on step one.

The Strike Force knew Group 504 existed. They knew a lot about their goals and a little about their methods. But it's real hard to get them for whatever crimes they're into until you know where they are. It has to be something more specific than "Reliable intelligence indicates a possible base of operation on the northwest coastal area, possibly northern California."

So Chandler had to start from nothing.

Locate them. Find the bastards. Without violating anybody's goddamn rights. That's where the search warrant came in.

Weeks of investigation had led them to Kenneth "Buffalo" Branson. Buffalo had committed his first major felony, apart from a string of car thefts and burglaries, at the tender age of fifteen. He had killed a drug dealer during an argument about the division of proceeds from a narcotics sale. He was released on his sixteenth birthday, after seven months in the Youth Authority.

Buffalo hadn't wasted the seven months. It had given him a master's degree in crime, and he was ready to go for a doctorate.

Within a few years he was back in the joint. This time it was a couple of counts of manslaughter. It should have been first-degree murder. That's what the prosecutor asked for. But Branson and his crime partner, Crank Krasne, had testified sincerely that the killings had occurred over a sudden quarrel, rather than the planned executions they really had been. Branson's lawyer, a female public defender, even had tears in her eyes when she asked the jury for a verdict of not guilty.

The jury, gullible but well-meaning, hadn't wanted to go quite that far and had returned verdicts of voluntary manslaughter. As far as Branson and Krasne were concerned, that was a victory.

When he got out, he had his Ph.D., and then some. These days he ran a string of labs that manufactured illegal methamphetamine, "crank" in the street parlance. The meth was produced under Buffalo's supervision and distributed by members or associates of outlaw motorcycle gangs.

The proceeds reportedly went to the White Knights, generally in the form of automatic weapons. The Buffalo had connections.

Chandler also knew how to use the weapons himself. Moreover, he liked to. It added a certain pucker-factor to the prospect of serving a search warrant on his house.

On the surface, of course, Branson looked respectable enough. He was employed as a bouncer at a topless bar, though in fact he was a shadow owner of the place. It also served as a hub where pound-quantities of meth were distributed. Branson rode his chopper occasionally, listened to country and western music and participated in toy drives for the poor at Christmas.

All of which was a front, but it paid big dividends in PR—it could be a hell of an ace in the hole the next time he faced a judge or jury.

The Strike Force headquarters were in the office section of an old warehouse in East L.A. Everybody from file clerks to computer operators had been cleared top secret. The agents talked to informants, pored over reports, sifted through rumor and hearsay to find the kernels of hard evidence. And now, finally, it was about to pay dividends. They hoped.

At 8:40 the door opened. Chandler, who had been going over the search warrant for perhaps the hundredth time, turned around to greet the new agents.

He found himself looking into the cold blue eyes of Carl Lyons.

Behind Lyons stood Blancanales and Schwarz. The Ironman, the Politician and Gadgets.

Chandler stared at them. In court he had the reputation of being ready for anything, impossible to throw off stride. But at this moment his mind refused to accept the data his eyes were sending.

"Holy shit!" he exclaimed at last.

"Morning, Counselor," Lyons responded with a grin. "Is that a legal term?"

The prosecutor shook his head in disbelief. "Holy shit," he repeated.

"SO WHAT'S THE PLAN, MIKE?" The introductions and how-the-hell-are-you's over, Lyons was chafing to get to work.

Chandler nodded to a back room. "We've got a diagram of the house. Come on, I'll show you."

The second room was as plain as the first. Old asphalt tile that was turning brown with age covered the floor. A couple of heavy wood tables, their tops scarred from years of government service, were littered with papers and reports. The chairs were ancient wooden beasts. Taped to one wall was a large, hand-drawn diagram of a house. Next to it was a black-and-white enlargement of an aerial photograph of the same residence.

"Where'd you come up with the furniture?" Blancanales inquired. "It looks like something out of an old movie."

"Except for the computers," agreed Gadgets.

Chandler nodded. "Most of it came out of government storage. It's probably forty years old. The filing cabinets and the computer terminals are about the only new stuff here. Oh, and the air conditioners. Even the coffeepot is an antique; one of the guys picked it up at a garage sale."

"I thought the Justice Department had money to burn," observed Lyons.

"If they do, we haven't seen it. Besides, it takes six months to requisition anything. Easier to do it this way."

Chandler waved them into chairs. "We'll be having a formal briefing this afternoon. For now, here's what we've got." He gestured at the diagram and the aerial photo on the wall.

"The house is a damn fortress. It wasn't built that way, but it's been reinforced."

"How so?" inquired Blancanales.

Chandler pointed to a picture. "The brick facing on the front is real brick, not just some kind of facade. The doors are solid oak, and the windows are barred. It won't be easy to get inside."

"I don't know about that," said Blancanales with a wink. "We could just hit the thing with a couple of grenades, or maybe a LAW rocket. That'll get us inside."

Chandler grinned. "Yeah, it would. Unfortunately, my job is to make a case for court, not for the coroner. Which reminds me . . ."

"Yes?" said Lyons.

"Just why are you guys here?"

"What do you mean?"

"Come off it," retorted the prosecutor. "This is way out of your line, and we both know it. What gives?"

"Didn't they tell you?"

"No. All I heard is they were sending me three additional men. They didn't give any names, much less why three, uh, specialized types such as yourselves would be the ones."

"We have a mutual interest," Lyons replied.

"Group 504?"

"Affirmative."

"What's your interest in them?" inquired the prosecutor.

"Well, for one thing, I believe they're responsible for the recent death of a sort of an old friend of mine."

"That business yesterday? The hijacking?"

Lyons nodded.

"I'm sorry," Chandler said simply.

"Yeah. Anyway, that's only part of it. The smallest part."

"So, what's the rest?"

Lyons grinned. "I'm interested because my boss says I'm interested. 'Orders is orders,' and all that sort of crap. He points, I march. It's the mission."

Chandler thought it over. Gradually an outline began to form in the mists. "What are your instructions?"

"Why, to assist you in your investigation," said Lyons blandly.

"To help get them legally," agreed Blancanales.

"We've been practicing," chimed in Gadgets.

"Practicing?"

"Yep." Gadgets stood up and pantomimed a machine gun. He raked a roomful of imaginary targets with the weapon then said, " 'Halt. You're all under arrest.' " Turning to Chandler, he asked, "That's how it goes, right?"

Chandler put his head in his hands. Without looking up, he replied, "Sort of. Generally we tell them they're under arrest *before* shooting, though."

"I never can keep that straight," said Gadgets, shaking his head.

"So I've noticed."

"Before, after, what's the difference?" asked Blancanales.

Lyons grinned at the spectacle. Then he got serious. "Actually, those *are* our orders. We've been temporarily assigned to your team. We were told to assist you in getting them legally. If possible."

"And if not possible?"

"We improvise, I guess."

Chandler thought it over. The outline in the mist was starting to look clearer by the minute.

Somebody in the Justice Department was being cute. Real cute.

Able Team wasn't there by accident. They were directed to be there by somebody in the upper echelons of the Justice Department. It had to be somebody who knew about Stony Man, or at least about Able Team. Whoever it was had to know about the Strike Force, as well. Finally, whoever it was had to have the power to bring the two together.

That meant somebody very high up, indeed. It also meant somebody wanted Group 504 taken out, never mind the cost, and never mind the methods.

A lot of things began to make sense; such as why he, Mike Chandler, was tagged for this particular operation.

There had been plenty of experienced prosecutors who could have been chosen. These Strike Force positions were regarded as plums. They were prestigious appointments that normally went to people with a lot of political clout and a hell of a lot of ability. The men assigned to all the other teams had both.

Mike knew he had the ability. He also knew that he didn't have the clout. Moreover, he had been the only state D.A. chosen; the rest of the appointees had been Feds. What, then, did he have that a hundred other would-be strike force attorneys didn't have? There was only one thing that he could think of—the ability to try it legally, and if that failed, then to not balk at other methods.

Methods that went beyond the law. Methods that involved the likes of Able Team.

That had to be it. Try it the right way. Then, if necessary, fall back to something else.

He'd done it before. Now, looking at the men of Able Team and adding up the facts in his strategist's mind, he knew somebody wanted him to do it again.

7

The 0530 grayness hung over Los Angeles like a dismal shroud. It never ceased to amaze Lyons that the morning could look so colorless, yet in a couple of hours it would be bright and hot.

For now, though, the gray added to the tingle of excitement. In half an hour they would hit the house.

The search warrant was signed, sealed and delivered. They would go through the legal formalities of "knock/notice" to keep the judges happy, but they had added a wrinkle or two of their own.

"I'm a little rusty on the procedures," Lyons had observed during the briefing held the previous afternoon. "You still have to '844' the door?"

"Well, this is a federal warrant, rather than a state one," Chandler responded. "Strictly speaking, Section 844 applies only to California State search warrants."

"But?"

"We have to do a similar procedure, anyway. Besides, depending on what we find inside, it's possible the case would be prosecuted in state court, anyway."

"Even though it's a federal warrant? You can do that?"

Chandler nodded. "Yes. But it means we have to go through the whole knock/notice routine under Section 844. So we're going to."

Lyons shook his head disgustedly. "Let's see. These guys are associates of one of the most dangerous terrorist groups in the country. They are paramilitary freaks, heavy into automatic weapons. Who knows but they could be the ones responsible for the five murders yesterday—two of them cops. Am I right so far?"

"Basically, yes," acknowledged the prosecutor.

"And we're going to walk up to the front door like good little cops. We'll have our search warrant in hand. We knock politely on the door. Then we announce nice and loud, 'police officers with a search warrant—open up.' Do I have this right?"

"What can I say? It's the law." Chandler's voice showed his irritation.

"Does the law make us bulletproof?"

Nobody tried to reply. Finally the silence was broken by Jack Hogan, the deputy sheriff from San Diego.

At five foot ten and 210 pounds, Hogan had the heavily muscled shoulders of a power-lifter, which indeed he had once been. He had a soft, hoarse voice, the result of a bullet fragment he'd taken in the throat a few years back. He didn't talk much. When he did, it was usually worth hearing. Lyons had realized immediately that Hogan was a pro.

"There may be another way."

The others looked at him. He continued, his voice sounding thoughtful. "What about flash-bangs?"

Chandler looked over at him. "What do you mean?"

"Controlled-emission grenades. When it goes off in a room, the concussion from the blast temporarily stuns whoever's inside. The light from the flash blinds them, again only temporarily."

"How long is temporarily?" inquired the prosecutor.

"A few seconds to a couple of minutes. It depends on the conditions. Long enough to make entry."

"Have you used those before? On searches?"

Hogan nodded. "A couple of times. It involves a certain amount of risk, of course. But sometimes it's the lesser of two evils, so to speak."

Chandler looked around. "Anybody else familiar with these things?"

Able Team, of course, was. One of the U.S. marshals and the CIA man also nodded their heads. The others made no sign.

"All right, let's kick that idea around a little," the prosecutor agreed.

The final plan was simple. A backup team would cover the house, one man on each side at the rear corners; one man in the back.

A six-man entry team would hit the front door. Two would be on the battering ram. The others would be in two teams of two, behind the men on the ram. When the door gave way, they would be first inside. The men with the ram would follow.

The key to the entry would be the flash-bangs.

They finally decided on using two of them. One would go in the main bedroom; a second in the living room. When everybody was ready, Chandler would make the legal announcement. When he finished, the grenadiers would punch a hole in the respective windows and drop their toys inside.

"How will the entry team know when to go into action?" asked Lyons with a wink.

"Watch for when the windows are blown out," Hogan replied, deadpan. "You might also be able to hear it."

"Oh."

"Theoretically, nothing inside will be moving until we get the place secured."

"Let's hope you're right."

They staged at 0500 the next morning at an abandoned gas station two blocks away from the house. The air seemed especially calm at that time of day, the quiet broken only by the mechanical sounds of an occasional car or truck.

Lyons felt a peculiar sense of distortion. His cop days were gone forever, yet the situation—the search warrant, the bright yellow raid vests with the single word Police stenciled in black letters across the back, the tension and the muted banter to ease it—stirred old memories.

Memories of triumphs and defeats. Memories of lost loves and lost lives, of times and people and things that had come and were gone, some of them forever.

Somebody once said that a man's life was the sum total of his experiences. As a rule, Lyons didn't believe in going back to check the math. Today, though, for some reason he found himself doing just that.

Lyons hadn't smoked for years, but he accepted a cigarette from one of the U.S. marshals, anyway. It tasted awful, but it was symbolic, another token from the past.

In making the assignments, Chandler had to balance what he knew were Able Team's combat skills with the fact that they were newcomers to the team.

"Ironman, you'll be on the 'key' with Hogan."

Blancanales looked at Lyons, puzzled. "The key?" he inquired.

"The battering ram," Lyons added.

"Oh." Blancanales gave his easy grin in an effort to hide the fact that for once he had embarrassed himself.

Chandler went on. "Pol, I want you and Gadgets to handle the flash-bangs on the east side of the house. That's the back bedroom. Adams and Johnston," he gestured at two of the other men, "will do the honors on the living room."

They nodded; the prosecutor went on, making the other assignments, calling out the strike force members to be the first through the door and to cover the sides and back of the house.

"Any questions?" Chandler asked at last.

There weren't any.

"All right, then. We'll hold here for ten more minutes, then move in and take up our positions. Good luck." He resisted the temptation to add "and be careful out there."

Lyons checked his gear for the last time. In his police days he had carried either a Colt Python .357 Magnum revolver or one of the Smith & Wesson counterparts, usually a Model 19. Today, it was the latter, a workhorse service weapon in blue steel with a four-inch barrel.

Lyons knew that cops and soldiers often fell prey to the same vices where their guns were concerned. Either they fell in love with their guns or, incredibly, they ignored them.

Lyons allowed himself to do neither. Guns were tools of the trade, and he selected them accordingly.

He removed the snazzy polished wood grips and installed black rubber Pachmeyers. The rubber grips had a tacky, almost sticky feel that seemed to grab your hand back when you grabbed them. It made for better accuracy and weapon retention.

The ammo was 125-grain jacketed hollowpoint. That round in the .357 Magnum cooked out of the muzzle at over 1400 feet per second and had an expansion factor that opened a hell of a hole in whatever it hit. Even more importantly, Lyons knew the round and was comfortable with it.

He wore body armor, a Kevlar vest, under his shirt. Next came the raid jacket and over that the shoulder holster with the Model 19. He carried two speed loaders of extra ammo on his belt and twelve more rounds in plastic speed strips in his trouser pocket.

Except for the weaponry, the other men were similarly attired. In addition to the raid vests, each wore a blue baseball cap with the word Police in gold letters across the crown. Blancanales carried a Government Model .45, while Gadgets had the same gun in 9 mm.

"So, what do you think, Ironman?" Gadget's voice was low. As he spoke, he stepped next to Lyons and leaned with his back against the van to keep their conversation private.

Lyons shrugged. "We'll soon see, I guess."

There was a pause, then Gadgets continued. "I don't like it."

"What do you mean?"

"I don't know. Something just doesn't feel right, you know?"

Lyons looked at his partner. If most people had said that, he would have written them off as nervous or as amateurs, or both. But not Gadgets. The man had a sixth sense that was uncanny. Besides, he had been right on target too many times for Lyons to ignore.

Added to it were his own disquieting feelings. Maybe it wasn't all nostalgia. Maybe it was part of what Gadgets had sensed.

"Spell it out."

"I can't."

"Thanks a lot. Maybe you're just not used to playing by the rules. After all—" Lyons grinned as he spoke "—you haven't had too much practice arresting people."

Gadgets shrugged. "What can I say? But you're going through the door, not me. Watch yourself."

Lyons grinned and discarded the last third of the cigarette. "Always, pal. Always."

LYONS AND HOGAN moved silently into position at the front door.

They held the "key" between them. It had begun life as the drive shaft on a cement mixer. When it retired from that, it was modified to its present use.

Four crude handholds, each made of reinforcing rod, or "re-bar," as Hogan called it, had been welded onto the shaft. The handles resembled six-inch *D*s and were located opposite each other, two toward the front and two toward the rear. A large blunt head, some ten inches across, was welded on one end. The head was backed up by a core of iron—six ten-pound weight-lifting plates that somebody had filched from the LAPD gym. It brought the total weight of the tool to just over a hundred pounds.

A man on each side, and the key was ready to go. By swinging it between them, a couple of strong men could open most doors. It should make short work of even a solid oak door like the one on Branson's place.

Lyons had noted with amusement that some wit had gone to the expense and trouble of having raised letters, backward of course, welded onto the end of the head.

The letters said LAPD—Los Angeles Police Department. That made it a hundred-pound stamping tool, ready to leave its mark wherever it struck. Lyons could relate to that— good cops were the same everywhere.

Silently Lyons and Hogan took up their position at the front door, the ram between them. The primary entry team poised behind them, weapons out and ready. The others slipped into position to the sides and behind the house.

The tension was gone. In its place was an adrenaline rush, the excitement of battle, the prospect of combat.

It was a knowledge that they better win, because if they lost, they lost big. And if they lost, it would be now, at the entry, when they were vulnerable and exposed as they went into the enemy's turf.

The higher the stakes, the more seductive the risk.

Lyons was aware of Blancanales and Gadgets moving swiftly and silently across the street. They ran in a low crouch, each wearing a heavy leather glove and gripping the flash-bang grenades that Hogan had supplied. They were good ones, Lyons had seen, manufactured in Belgium by FFE. Each would generate a million candela, and noise in the range of eighty decibels.

If that didn't do it, nothing would.

Chandler poised to make the 844 announcement.

Three steps until battle, Lyons thought. Three steps and we're in for the duration.

The announcement would come "Police officers—we have a search warrant—open up, *now!*"

Then flash-bangs, and entry.

Simple. Just like that. Killers to be captured in the early morning cool.

Chandler raised his megaphone to make the announcement. Lyons gathered himself to make the assault with the key.

As he did so, they heard a noise from inside the house. It was the telephone ringing.

8

Tami Bonner eased the little Mustang into her reserved parking space at the Federal building. It was two hours earlier than she normally arrived for work.

"Mornin', Miss Bonner." The security guard at the front counter, a retired postal contractor named Vern Thorson, smiled as he pushed the sign-in log over toward her. Of Norwegian descent, he had ham-size forearms and powerful, sloping shoulders, the result of years of slinging heavy mail sacks, four at a time. "You're here bright and early."

"Hi, Vern. I've got a bunch of paperwork to catch up on."

"Well, you have a good day."

"You, too." She signed her name and entered "time in" 5:40 A.M., using a circle to dot the *i* in Tami, and making a stylized "happy face" in the zero of the *time*.

He smiled again. "For me, the day's almost over."

"Have a good night, then."

Vern watched appreciatively as she walked to the elevators. She was pert and girlish, with slim legs and high young breasts that had made her a favorite at the Fox 'n' Goose, the topless bar where she had worked before becoming a clerk at the Federal Courthouse.

Upstairs, Tami turned on the lights and started to make some coffee. Then, humming lightly to herself, she set about doing what she was paid to do.

Unofficially. Under the table. In addition to her check from the U.S. Government.

She began to peruse the search warrants signed the previous day.

Usually, she did it on her lunch hour. It was ridiculously easy, since security was so lax. She had a list of names to watch out for. If she found any that were on the list, she made a telephone call. The information wound up at the office of a prominent criminal defense attorney. In return, an envelope of cash somehow appeared in her car a few days later.

Sometimes she felt bad about it.

She had gotten to know some of the agents who were obtaining the warrants, and a lot of them were nice. She felt sorry for them when their cases were ruined. But that's what the Buffalo told her to do, and that's what she would do.

He was a cruel bastard. But he was her old man, and he owned her.

Besides, that same lawyer had gotten Branson off on a big beef. He had also gotten her the job at the courthouse.

What the hell? If she didn't do it, somebody else probably would.

She scanned the new warrants. Nothing of interest. Then she saw one that was sealed in an envelope. The name of the judge was stamped across the sealed flap.

That was a judge's idea of security. Sign it, seal it, and put your name across the seal.

Nonchalantly she tore it open. She had access to an identical manila envelope—no tough project since they were standard U.S. Government supply—and a name stamp with the judge's name.

The sheaf of papers inside was thick. A boldface heading leaped out at her: United States Department of Justice—

Interagency Strike Force. She saw the name Mike Chandler down at the bottom of the cover sheet.

"All right, guys," she said aloud to herself, "who are you and who're you after?"

She scanned the papers.

Her eyes widened as she read the name. It couldn't be. The coincidence was staggering. She read it again to be sure, and then checked the address to be double sure.

She picked up the telephone to make the first of what would be three telephone calls.

She didn't feel bad about it this time. After all, she was his old lady.

The plain round clock on the wall said eight minutes before six.

9

The telephone stopped in mid-ring. Had somebody inside answered it? Or had the caller hung up?

A curtain moved. A face showed at the front window then vanished. At the same time another man glanced out the side window where Blancanales was poised, grenade in hand, ready to reach between the window bars and punch his fist through the glass.

It was Branson.

Their instinct was to shoot. But the orders were to do it legally, so shooting was out, for the moment, anyway.

"Grenades!" Buffalo shouted the warning as he ducked back inside.

"We're burned!" Pol yelled to Chandler.

The prosecutor did the only thing he could. "Branson! This is the police! We have a warrant. Open the door." Then, to Pol and Gadgets, Chandler shouted, "Now!"

Lyons heard the sound of breaking glass. A measured second later, the twin blasts of the flash-bangs shook the building.

A searing sheet of white light flashed from the windows where Gadgets and Blancanales crouched after delivering the grenades. Glass shattered, showering them with fragments. The curtains bulged against the ornamental security bars.

"Now!" yelled Lyons to Hogan.

They heaved the ram backward then swung it forward against the oak door.

There was a security gate fashioned of wrought iron on the outside of the door. The bars twisted inward before the powerful blow. It flashed through Lyons's mind that if the bars caved in this easily, the door would be a piece of cake.

Except that when the bars smashed against the wooden door, it was like hitting a vault.

The impact jarred the two men. The bars had crumpled as they were pressed against the door. But the door didn't budge.

"Again!" snapped Lyons.

They heaved back and swung forward. The key struck with a force that shook the house. The door remained solidly in place.

Something was badly wrong. Even a heavy oak door like this one should have splintered under such concentrated force.

The hollow sound from the blow provided the answer. The door was metal—steel—set into a reinforced frame. The heavy wood exterior was just a covering.

"Again!" The word emerged as a roar between Lyons's clenched teeth. As the ram struck, the impact forced an explosive grunt from each man. The house shook.

Mentally, Lyons counted off the time. With each second that passed, the men inside would be recovering from the flash-bangs. If they came around, it would be sitting-duck time for the strike force members.

The two men worked in unison, using the rebound from each blow to help them set up for the next. The wood splintered away, leaving the heavy steel beneath it. Loud metallic clanks rang out as the ram struck home. Behind them the entry teams was poised, ready for the assault.

Suddenly the door buckled. Two more blows, and then a ragged gap appeared as the edge of the door sprung away from the frame. Then it burst open to reveal the smoke-filled living room. The chemical smell of burned ordnance washed over them.

"We've got it!" shouted Hogan.

Sweat soaked Lyons's shirt, even though the morning was not yet hot. Hogan released his grip on the ram and stepped to one side, out of the way. Lyons turned as he swung the heavy tool and heaved it off to one side. It dropped with a metallic clang to the sidewalk.

The entry teams burst past them into the house. Hogan was hard on their heels, gun in hand. Lyons drew the Magnum from his shoulder holster and started after them.

Automatic weapon fire erupted from within the house. The bright flashes cut through the eddying smoke from the flash-bangs.

Lyons knew the sound—9 mm. An Uzi, or something similar. Those guns had become almost standard issue for drug dealers everywhere.

Christ, but we're out-gunned, he thought.

Gun in hand, he dived inside at an angle, going in fast and low. With the soldier's instinct, he knew the burst wasn't meant for him. And, with the same sixth sense—the way that one person can be aware of another—he knew the entry team was dead.

A line of 9 mm slugs stitched a row of bloody dots and dashes up the body of the first U.S. marshal through the door. The high-speed bullets made little thuds of impact as they hit flesh. The man stumbled and fell across a cluttered glass coffee table.

Lyons snapped off a shot at the muzzle flashes as he dove for cover behind a couch. He landed almost on top of one of the entry men, but a choking scream from in front of him said that at least the shot was on target. He scrambled forward to where he could peer around the couch at his adversaries.

Suddenly the 9 mm fire increased. The sound was deafening in the confined space.

Lyons jerked back as a burst thudded into the couch. In one of those crazy details the mind records in the middle of a firefight, he saw little puffs of dust rise from the impact points.

The handguns carried by the entry team made a scattered response. The shots sounded pitiful and inadequate against the full-auto firepower wielded by Buffalo and his friends. The screams from the entry team confirmed it.

Lyons rolled out from behind the couch and emptied his revolver at the men ahead of him. Rolling back, he thumbed the cylinder open and dumped the six empties with his right hand, his left scrambling for the speed-loaders at his belt.

The old reflexes from his cop days took over as he reloaded.

From day one old Smitty, the range master at LAPD, had made the recruits dump their brass onto the dirt instead of into a coffee can. The same thing was mandatory for speed-loaders. Any man who did otherwise would be doing push-ups until his arms fell off.

There was a reason for this. Lyons had known it then, and it was still with him today, years later. The way you practice is the way you'll do it when it's for real. When the grim reaper is hovering off to one side, watching and waiting to take the souls of the dead, you don't worry about your speed-loader or brass getting dirty.

For your partner's sake, if not your own.

"Forget the brass!" Smitty had screamed into their faces. "Forget the fucking speed-loaders! You gonna worry about that in a shoot-out, you dip-shit?"

Lyons had learned well. Without a thought he twisted the speed-loader free and discarded it onto the ground.

At the same time he heard the click and clink of another clip being rammed home by one of the defenders. Another thirty rounds ready, compared to his own six.

I could die here, he suddenly thought.

It wasn't fear, just an abstract realization. It struck him as almost funny—after all the shit I've been through in every godforsaken hellhole on earth, I could eat the big one trying to arrest a dope dealer in a little three-bedroom tract house in the middle of L.A.

Something thumped onto the dirty carpet ahead of him. Even before he saw it, Lyons knew the sound could mean only one thing.

A grenade. It had been tossed by Buffalo or one of his buddies.

And it was a real one, not a flash-bang.

10

Pol had seen the face at the window as he crouched, ready to drop the flash-bangs after Gadgets punched the hole. He knew in an instant that it was Buffalo and shouted the warning.

He gripped the grenade in his right hand as he crouched, his left shoulder against the rough stucco wall. He wore a special glove—more of a gauntlet, actually—over his right hand. Made of wire mesh sandwiched between two layers of leather, it would protect his fist from any shards of glass that remained after Gadgets did his job.

"Stand by," he said to Gadgets.

"Ten-four."

His partner wore the other glove on his left hand. He crouched facing Blancanales, so that his left hand was free. On the signal from Chandler—the "now" at the end of the announcement telling Branson to open the door—Gadgets would rise and punch his fist between the bars and through the glass. Then he would duck to one side for Pol to deliver the payload.

In theory, there was another team doing the same thing to the other side of the house. The one-second fuses meant the blasts would be quick. It was hoped they would also be nearly simultaneous.

Chandler's voice over the loudspeaker cut the morning stillness. The two men tensed, ready to spring into action on the *go* word.

"Now!" they heard from the loudspeaker.

"Do it!" hissed Blancanales.

The command was unnecessary.

Gadgets rose slightly and drove his fist between the bars that covered the window. The thin glass shattered. He worked his fist in a quick circle, the wire mesh and leather of the heavy glove protecting him. Then he dragged his hand back between the bars, turning away and ducking to leave the path clear for Pol.

Catlike, Blancanales delivered the mail.

The two men crouched below the window, hugging the wall.

At least, that part of the operation went right. The blasts were virtually simultaneous. The wall shook from the concussion. A sheet of white light leaped from the window above them. Fragments of glass showered down.

"That should do the trick," the ever-cool Politician said with a wink.

"Are you sure that was only a flash-bang?"

"I hope so. We were supposed to do this legally, remember?"

"Yeah. Well, I doubt they'll be doing too much for a couple of minutes."

They had no idea how wrong they were.

INSIDE THE HOUSE, Branson, the munitions buff, had seen the grenade. In the two seconds it took Chandler to make the legal demand, the Buffalo leaped away from the window. He dove across the bed and against the far wall. His hands over his ears, mouth open to equalize the pressure from both sides of his eardrums, and eyes scrunched shut, he hugged the wall across from the window.

Branson's best friend (assuming he had any friends) was a tall, stringy biker nicknamed Slimy. He, too, was no stranger to munitions, having served in Vietnam. Nervous and edgy, still strung out from the methamphetamine he had taken, Slimy had been awakened by the telephone call.

He heard Branson's warning and reacted instantly, covering up and diving for cover.

The other two men in the small house were slower to react. The blinding light and concussion knocked them down and out.

In the ear-ringing aftermath of the blast, Buffalo and Slimy crawled groggily to their feet. A ringing blow from the front door told them a ram of some sort was being used. Seconds later the two men were armed.

Buffalo's eyes burned with hatred. "All right, pigs. Come and get it."

Slimy nodded his agreement. He jacked a round into the Mac 10. The trap was ready.

"WHAT THE HELL'S THE PROBLEM UP FRONT?" muttered Gadgets as the sound of the heavy, hollow blows reached them.

Both men knew the answer. There was nothing to do but wait.

Blancanales glanced at his watch. The sweep second hand was crossing the 4—twenty seconds after.

The blows continued. Then the sound changed, and they knew the door was yielding. The sweep hand was around to the 12; fifty seconds had elapsed. No problem. The effect of the flash-bangs would last longer than that.

Seconds later gunfire erupted from inside the house.

"Auto-burn!" snapped Blancanales. The term was a holdover from his days in Vietnam, where he had served in the elite 5th Special Forces group.

Gadgets didn't have to be told. He also knew what that meant to the men trying to get inside.

Death. The burning impact of bullets.

Blancanales leaped to his feet. He didn't know what to do, but he had to do something, had to get inside. Under other circumstances, it would have been no problem. A grenade—a real one—and then into the room through the hole. But he couldn't do that here, because this wasn't war.

Was it?

His eye caught the corner of the metal framework of bars. The heavy lag bolt that secured it to the stucco, and presumably to the framing beneath it, seemed to be loose. Pol grabbed it and gave a yank.

The bolt moved in the stucco. It didn't come free, but at least it moved.

He looked into the room. There was nobody there. The men inside the house must be toward the front. "Cover me!"

Blancanales reholstered his .45 and grabbed the iron bars with both hands. Aware that he was a sitting duck in the window, he yanked again.

Again the bars moved but didn't give.

Gripping the bars, he gave a little jump. In midair he brought his knees to his chest and braced his feet against the building. The powerful muscles of his legs tensed as he strained against the bars, the tension holding him in a crouchlike stance against the wall.

Gadgets moved swiftly to one side to cover the room.

For a long moment nothing happened. The bars flexed outward as Blancanales strained. Then the bolts pulled free, first the loose one then the one at the top corner. The grid of bars twisted outward and came free on all corners, except for one.

Blancanales fell heavily backward.

Gadgets grabbed the bars and twisted the frame, torquing it against the remaining bolt. Then he used the barrel of his Beretta to knock out any shards of glass that remained from the blast, running it along the interior of the frame.

He turned and held his hand down as a step for Blancanales. The former Green Beret stepped up and dove inside the room, helped by the boost. Gadgets scrambled in after him.

"Look out!" Gadgets shouted the warning as he dropped inside.

A figure appeared in the doorway, dazedly coming around after the explosion from the flash-bang. He held an automatic pistol in his hand and when he saw the two Able Team members, his gaze focused. The pistol came up and toward them.

Gadgets and Blancanales fired simultaneously. 9 mm and .45 caliber craters erupted on the man's dirty white T-shirt.

The Able Team veterans scrambled forward. Through the doorway leading to the hall they could see a skinny man leaning against the wall. He held a Mac 10 loosely in his hands. As they watched, the man took a hit. The gun sagged and the man's knees buckled. He slid slowly to the floor, leaving a bloody smear down the wall where the slug had torn a bloody exit wound in his back.

Near him crouched the Buffalo.

He, too, held a Mac 10. He fired on auto-burn, directing the bursts into the men struggling for cover in the smoky living room.

Was anybody still alive in there?

Branson's weapon emptied and locked open. He came up with a fresh clip and shoved it into place. Then from nowhere a grenade appeared in Branson's hand. Gadgets and Blancanales raised their pistols.

It all seemed to go down in slow motion. They couldn't get their guns up in time. The grenade arced into the living room, just as Gadgets's and Blancanales's Beretta and Colt opened up.

11

He didn't have to see it.

As he lay there on the worn carpet behind the couch, Lyons had known there was only one thing that could have made the thud on the rug ahead of him. Now, as he looked, he recognized it as an M-26 fragmentation grenade. Antipersonnel, deadly, it would fill the room with a storm of projectiles and fragments, not to mention the effect of the blast itself.

Time was running. Instantly his mind did the calculations.

Too close to get away from it.

Too far to get to it.

Something moved in his peripheral vision. It was a man-size shape that suddenly loomed up, off to one side. Instinctively, Lyons twisted toward the movement, ready to fire.

It was Hogan, the muscular deputy sheriff who had been on the ram with him.

Hogan had gone through the door right after the initial entry team, while Lyons was heaving the key off to one side. Then Lyons had drawn his gun and made his diving entry, just as Hogan was killed by the enemy inside.

Lyons had seen it happen. The sheriff's man had absorbed an entire burst from the 9 mm ahead of them.

It had been a prolonged burst. Dead center. Lyons could hear the impact of the bullets over the din of the gunfire.

The body armor might have stopped the first and second and third slugs and maybe even a couple after that. But at some point, those that followed would chew their way through the resilient material. And besides, penetrate or not, each round would deliver its full four-hundred-odd foot-pounds of energy to the tissue and organs beneath it.

Lyons had seen the heavily muscled officer stagger as he took the hits. Hogan still drove forward, but the coordination was somehow gone. It was as though momentum rather than purpose was now what carried him. Then the message had gotten through—you're dead—and he'd gone down at last.

Scratch one hell of a good man.

Lyons could feel that the next bullets had his own name on them, except that the single diving shot he had snapped off foiled the plan.

But Hogan was on his feet again. Somehow, his mind hadn't accepted the fact that he was dead.

The mental computer had said "input error" when the nerves flashed up "you're dead." The will to live had over-ridden the physics of energy transference to flesh and blood. Hogan had rejected the data, had chosen not to obey the natural laws of wound ballistics.

And now, incredibly, he had put himself back in the game for one final down.

As the deputy lurched forward, Lyons could see the devastation the gunfire had wrought. The yellow raid jacket was torn to pieces in the chest area, as was the Kevlar vest beneath it. The body armor now looked like a bloodsoaked sponge, as dreadful as if it were part of the man's flesh.

Nobody survived that much damage. Hogan was dead. He had died when he took that burst.

For a split second his eye met Lyons's. And in that instant Hogan did something that would stay with the Ironman the rest of his life.

He winked.

With that one gesture Hogan communicated everything that could ever be noble about the human spirit. Love. Courage. Goodness. Doing an act for no better reason than that it was right.

And there was something else in that look, as well—a glint of cynical amusement, a rueful "what the hell" from one man to another.

Then he plunged forward, half diving, half falling, in a clumsy tackle aimed at the grenade.

He landed full-length on the floor, the bomb just beyond his outstretched arm. He grabbed for it and missed. Then he somehow heaved himself forward, and the grenade was in his hand. He pulled it to himself, curling his bloodsoaked body around it, tucking it against his sternum at the V where his ribs met, so the explosion would be shielded primarily by the heavier meat and bones of his chest rather than the softer viscera of his abdomen....

12

In northern California, some three or four hundred miles above Los Angeles, a telephone rang at a couple of minutes before 6:00 A.M.

It had been long-distance from L.A. The call lasted seven minutes.

The man who answered the telephone replaced the receiver gently. Clad only in his undershorts, he sat on the edge of his bed and thought over what he had just learned.

It was not good news.

He was a powerful man of about forty. Thick dark brown hair hung down to his meaty shoulders. He wore a heavy beard that showed a decidedly red tinge. His arms were massive, bloated with a musculature born of a combination of large doses of anabolic steroids—the so-called muscle drugs—and untold hours of straining against heavy weights.

Tattoos ran down his arms like lurid bruises.

The right bicep showed a screaming eagle. It was attacking a purple dragon that was tattooed on the forearm, beneath the eagle.

A gaping skull dominated the left arm.

It was on the outside of the upper arm, distorted somewhat by the swollen muscles, biceps in front and triceps to the rear. The skull was tipped back, as though looking upward in abject agony. It resembled something out of a Vesalius anatomy text.

A tangle of snakes struggled on the forearm. One, slightly bigger than the rest, was escaping the others. It crawled up the arm and into the skull at the triangular underside of the jawbone.

The man sat very still, thinking. Outside there was nothing but forest for miles. The rural stillness of the northern California wine and marijuana country dripped from an early morning fog.

He felt sluggish, his head heavy from the drugs and booze of the preceding evening. Under other circumstances he would have gone back to bed and not get up for another three hours. Today, however, the telephone call had pulled him awake. It had also sobered him faster than anything else could have done.

Finally he got stiffly to his feet. Beside him a blond woman stirred in the bed.

"Crank?" Her voice was thick with sleep. "Whazza matter, honey?"

"Nothin', babe. Little trouble in L.A., that's all."

"You getting up?" Said in a querulous voice, it sounded like a complaint.

Crank didn't answer. Instead he walked through the door into the bathroom. He turned on the shower and waited for the warm water. Then gingerly he stepped out of his shorts and under the hot spray.

The warmth began to sweep the mud from his brain.

"Trouble in L.A." was right. Some kind of state/federal investigation. "Interagency Strike Force," she had called it.

He muttered a curse. That was bad news all the way.

The armored car heist was bound to bring a lot of heat, of course. And two cops dead would mean max heat.

But he had been prepared for that. No clues—the trail would be impossible for the authorities to follow. Even if there were any witnesses, and he knew there weren't, the Happy Baby truck and all the firearms had ceased to exist.

The truck was already part of a cube of scrap metal. An hour after the money was off-loaded, the vehicle had been crushed into a sandwich between other dead cars at a nearby wrecking yard. Now it was awaiting transport to a recycling plant.

The weapons were in the ocean.

There would never be any clue to their vehicle or equipment. Sure, it was expensive, but with seven million dollars to play with, how did it matter? It was better than getting caught.

His dead soldiers had been less easy to dispose of. But he'd done it, and they would never be found—unless somebody dug up a stretch of freeway that was right now being paved with eight inches of concrete.

Three men dead.

There should have been none. The way it was planned and executed was perfect, except for one thing. That second cop had been too damn quick.

It was just bad luck. Most cops, out of shape or trying to work after a night of beer and partying, couldn't have reacted fast enough. And besides, most of them didn't have the training or instincts to react to a situation like this.

Except this one did.

"Fuckin' guy was pretty good," he muttered begrudgingly as he thought of the rugged officer.

Gingerly he touched his own chest. He winced when he found the spot. It was on the lowest rib on the left-hand side, a couple of inches below the slablike pectoral muscles. His fingers explored the tenderness.

He'd taken two rounds there.

That goddamn pig had hung in there to the very end. He had even managed to reload then get off a couple of shots just as Crank opened up with the M-16.

And they had been dead-on, just like the ones that had killed Shorty and Dirt-bag and L.A. Dave.

The only thing that had saved Crank was the body armor. That, and maybe several years of bombing his chest with heavy bench presses.

And now Tami calls with this strike force business. For them to have gotten a warrant on the Buffalo's place meant they already had an investigation well underway.

That was bad—and good.

The good part was that it had to be a coincidence that the warrant was coming along at this point. There was no way the Feds could suspect a connection between Buffalo and the killings yesterday.

The bad news was the timing. It was too close for comfort. The last thing he wanted was any law-enforcement action coming down on anybody associated with him until matters cooled down.

Whenever he was involved in something superillegal, Crank stuck to the letter of the law on everything else. He knew too many men who had fallen because they committed some minor infraction that led to the discovery of the big crimes.

Crank gave the faucet an abrupt twist to the right. Then he leaned forward, elbows on the tiled wall of the shower, bracing himself for the shock as the water turned cold.

It felt like needles of ice that lanced into his shoulders and back. The impact nearly took his breath away. He gasped and forced the air in and out of his lungs. Just when he couldn't stand it any longer, the water turned warm again.

"Move over."

Crank pushed back from the wall and saw the blonde. He moved stiffly to one side to let her in. As she stepped under the water, it cascaded off her head and slicked her long hair into a wide strip down her neck and the middle of her back.

His eyes fell to her back. Several long red marks ran across it. They had been inflicted the previous evening. If Crank's women wanted his drugs, and what support he gave them, they learned to put up with his rough stuff.

His groin tightened as he saw the welts. He turned her toward him.

She kept her eyes averted. He reached behind her neck and gripped a fistful of hair. Then he twisted his hand and levered her face up to his.

Her eyes were scared. That excited him even more. The dusky shadow of a bruise lay under her jaw on the right side, another souvenir of last night. He tightened the clench of his fist in her hair, pulling her head still farther backward. Then he gave a quick disciplinary jerk with his hand and released the hair.

She looked away again.

Crank's eyes narrowed dangerously. Using his thumb and forefinger, he gripped her jaw. Abstractly, he watched the cords of his forearm move under the skin as he tightened the grip. His thumb dug into the bruise.

A squeak of pain broke from her twisted lips.

He increased the pressure, turning her face to meet his. She made a thin high keening sound. Crank pushed his face into hers.

"Be a good girl." His voice was dead, deadly. Tears swam in her eyes. Unable to speak, she gave a little nod.

"Good."

He turned her loose. She caught her breath in a single iccupping sob then lowered herself to her knees before him.

As he watched her head work back and forth, Crank wondered idly who had made it possible for the Strike Force to get a warrant on Buffalo Branson. That there was a leak he had no doubt. Who it might be was a tougher question. Never mind—there was only one way to deal with snitches. Last guy he suspected of talking to the cops ended up with his neck broken by Crank's massive arms.

The memory excited him. He gripped her head in both hands and guided it at an ever-increasing tempo.

Someday, he thought, he'd kill her.

A LITTLE WHILE LATER Crank picked up the telephone and punched in a series of digits.

Things were worse than he imagined. He'd just gotten a call from Red Schaffley. If what Red told him was true, the cops were already at the Buffalo's place.

That meant extreme measures were called for.

The number was in Los Angeles. He had to make sure that no more leaks occurred, and because the best defense was a good offense, that meant plugging them up before they ever happened.

He had foreseen the possibility, of course. Informants were the standard tool of the police and prosecutors. Under normal circumstances, it didn't matter—his lawyers could always argue entrapment and violation of constitutional rights until—nine times out of ten—it just ended up costing him a few weeks' dope profits in fines and attorney fees.

But this was different. This wasn't just some million-dollar drug deal. It they got burned on this one, they just might not get away with dicking the case around until the jury let them go.

If he fell on this one, it would be death-penalty time. *If* he made it to trial.

Just as important, the cause would be set back immeasurably. And that mustn't happen. It was too important. Important for freedom. For America. For Crank Krasne.

The Fourth of July was coming. And when it arrived, the President of the United States would die.

He had to die.

Unlike the one before him, this President was a tough, no-bullshit guy. Under his leadership the climate of government didn't favor groups like Krasne's, the organized criminal enterprises that thrived outside the law.

This President had given back the CIA and the FBI their powers. He had focused the Justice Department's efforts on organized crime instead of environmental protection and women's causes. Hell, he had even expanded the use of wiretaps, and there were signs he was starting to go after the lawyers who helped to plan the crimes before they happened and defended the criminals afterward.

That would be devastating. Like a good whore, a good attorney could make all the right motions and could convince you that it was okay to be doing what you were doing.

It was a war. The target was named, and the target date was in sight. They couldn't risk a setback now. That meant eliminating any possible leak.

The man he was about to call would be the one to do it. He had been literally on standby to kill any possible informant in connection with the armored car caper and to kill himself if he got caught. Well, he could do the same thing now. In fact, he didn't even have to know that the search warrant probably wasn't related to the heist.

The phone was picked up on the first ring. "M.D. here."

M.D. was always there, thought Crank disgustedly. The guy's a psycho, but trustworthy. A useful tool, and one that Crank needed now.

"M.D., it's me."

"Whaddya need, boss?"

"You, M.D."

"Say it, man."

Crank chose his next words carefully. The line should be clear on his end, but no telling about the Los Angeles end.

"Looks like something may be coming down at Buffalo's place. Somethin' official. Ya know what I mean?"

"Right on."

"I don't want to take the chance that some asshole might snitch us off. I want you to check that out. Like we talked about in connection with that other thing. You remember?"

"Like we talked about? Buffalo and them others? You want me to handle it like that? *Exactly* like we talked about?"

"Just exactly like that."

"I got ya." M.D.'s tone of voice showed that he understood.

"Good. Call me later."

"Be easy, boss." The connection broke abruptly as M.D. hung up.

As Crank put down the telephone, he could picture what was going on at M.D.'s place.

The psycho would be unlocking a heavy gun safe in the closet of his house. He would be taking out a couple of guns, a scoped .30-06, probably, as well as an M-16 and a sidearm of some sort. A nylon bag would already have ammunition for each, and a second bag would be loaded with food and water. Inside of two minutes, M.D.'s old blue van could be on the road for Buffalo's place.

And when it got there, he would stake it out. Knowing M.D., if it took a week before the cops hit the place with the warrant, M.D. would wait that long. He would keep going on a combination of psychotic energy and ever-increasing lines of crank-crystal methamphetamine—that was the mainstay of all outlaw bikers.

M.D. would take care of anybody arrested by the cops. And, if it became necessary, he would take care of himself.

It was an extreme measure. Branson was tough and loyal, but one way or the other he was a dead man. Where cops were killed, the stakes were just too high to take the risk.

This was that—and more—though Branson didn't know the second part. Extreme measures were justified.

This Fourth of July would be one to remember.

Independence Day. Courtesy of himself, Crank Krasne.

13

Lyons pushed himself stiffly to his feet.

He didn't look at Hogan, or more accurately, what was left of him. But a collage of life and death remained, and would remain forever, in the recesses of Lyons's mind—the scrabbling reach; the powerful dying body curling around the grenade. The muffled "whump!" that lifted him off the floor...

Gun down at his side, Lyons walked slowly outside. It was only then that he saw it, the fine peppering of red clinging to the sun-baked hairs of his right forearm. Abstractly he realized that arm must not have been shielded when he covered up.

Hogan.

You're not dead until the last man who remembers you dies.

Lyons deliberately restrained the impulse to wipe off his arm. There would be time for that later.

Mike Chandler hurried up the walk and pushed by him into the living room. He surveyed the carnage for only a second. Then he turned to one of the federal agents and snapped out an order.

"MDT! Code three!"

"Roger." The agent sprinted for the car radio. Outside a crowd gathered on the sidewalk, looking and pointing and whispering. Sirens wailed in the distance.

The initials stood for Major Disaster Team. It was a standby apparatus used in any high-risk federal law enforcement effort. Chandler had made the proper notifications prior to obtaining the warrant.

When the MDT responded, a lot of things happened at once. The local authorities were notified, and a liaison set up to coordinate efforts.

Medical aid, ambulances or helicopters, as needed, would already be on standby. At the signal they would be dispatched.

Fire trucks, if necessary, could also be sent.

Then, after the initial life-saving measures were done, the process of sorting out what had happened would begin. Generally, the local cops would handle scene and crowd control and designate one or two investigators to work alongside the Feds in processing the scene.

Only after those wheels had been set in motion did Chandler ask the big question.

"What happened?"

"Somebody tipped them." Lyons's voice was hard, angry.

"Then what?"

"The goddamn door was steel underneath the oak. When we finally got inside, they started shooting."

"Body count?" Chandler had been in Vietnam himself, at a time when his Ivy League friends had been ducking the draft or going to work in defense plants. Lyons recalled that Chandler's path had even crossed Mack Bolan's in the jungles of Southeast Asia, and that the prosecutor was a tough and competent fighter.

"There were four of them. All dead."

"How about us?"

"The same. And one more probable." Lyons gestured with his head to an FBI agent. The man had been carried outside, and was being tended to by Blancanales, Able Team's medic. But Lyons could see the outlook wasn't good for the wounded man.

Chandler grimaced. "That's not too good."

"They had the high ground. Plus, we lost the element of surprise."

"I see." Chandler looked detached, remote. "It must have been that telephone call," he mused aloud. "Anybody hear what was said? Anything that might tell us if he was actually tipped about the raid, or whether he had been woken up and then happened to see us."

Nobody responded. Chandler nodded then turned on his heels and strode outside. Lyons followed him.

They went to the control van. Chandler keyed the microphone and spoke.

"Station G," he said simply, identifying himself.

"Go ahead, Station G. This is Station K," came the response.

"Give me a trace on the last call to subject phone."

"Stand by, G."

In a moment, the voice came back over the radio. "Unable to trace, Station G."

"What do you mean, unable to trace?" Chandler's voice had an edge to it.

"Call was made from a U.S. Government phone. All we get is the ID of the federal network. It could be one of ten thousand numbers."

"Are you sure?" Chandler demanded.

"Affirmative."

The prosecutor fell silent, stunned by the news. Then the radio spoke again.

"Station G? This is K. There's another call coming in right now."

"From the same number?"

"Negative."

"Give me a reading."

"Roger."

As Chandler spoke, Lyons sprinted for the house. He plunged inside and looked around for a phone.

The only one visible lay in the far corner of the living room, blasted there when the grenade went off. But the chirp of an electronic ring came from somewhere else in the house.

Lyons dashed down the hallway. Nothing, though the ring sounded louder. He burst into the nearest bedroom and scanned it quickly.

Still no phone. The ringer chirped again.

He whirled and started to go into the second bedroom. Something hauled him back, and then he knew where it was.

The bathroom.

He leaped inside and grabbed for it. It was a cheap plastic affair, the kind you buy and plug in yourself. Snatching it up, he grunted a single word.

"Yeah?"

"Buff? Buffalo? That you, buddy?" The voice sounded agitated, hyper.

On impulse, Lyons reached over and flushed the toilet. The water churned and gurgled. Hopefully, it would mask his voice.

"Yeah, man."

"Oh. It didn't sound like you. Look, man, Tami just called. The cops are probably on the way over to your place right now. They got a warrant. The Feds."

The voice stopped. Lyons knew what was going through the caller's mind. The monosyllabic grunts and the flushing toilet had thrown him off guard for a moment, but it was starting to add up. And what it undoubtedly added up to in the caller's mind was that it wasn't Branson he was talking to.

"Hey! Who is this? Who the fuck's on the phone?"

Lyons gave it a last try. "It's me, man. Buff—"

With a sharp click the connection was broken.

Lyons turned and sprinted back outside. Blancanales and Gadgets followed. They met Chandler at the van.

"Did you get a trace?" the Able Team leader demanded.

The prosecutor nodded.

"Where, for God's sake?"

Chandler handed Lyons a piece of paper on which he'd scrawled the address: 4557 Adams Avenue. Lyons looked at it for a long moment. Something was familiar, or at least, significant about it. Then he realized.

"Hell, I know where that is. It's in this same area. Can't be over a couple of miles."

Chandler nodded. He knew what was coming. Moreover, he didn't care.

Lyons jerked his head in the direction of their car, a dark blue Plymouth sedan. It was supposed to be an undercover car, but it looked so standardly plain that it might as well have been labeled "police vehicle, plainclothes model."

"Let's go!"

Gadgets and Blancanales piled inside. The prosecutor didn't try to stop them.

Nobody paid any attention to the battered blue van across the street. The driver, a thin man with long hair, leaned forward and started the engine. Slowly, at legal speed, the van pulled out and headed down the street after Able Team.

THEY FOUND 4557 without much difficulty. If anything, it was more run-down than Buffalo's place.

The house squatted desolately behind a patch of dried grass and dead weeds. It was a sorry, squalid affair, part stucco and part wood siding. The paint, a red-clay shade, had long since cracked and peeled from much of the wood; irregular cracks crisscrossed the stucco.

"You got a plan?" Blancanales had inquired of Lyons as they prowled the street, searching for the number.

"Who needs a plan?" The response was curt.

Blancanales recognized that Lyons was acting on sheer nervous fury. Out of respect for his comrade, he chose his words carefully, keeping his voice casual.

"All right, then. How should we do it?"

Lyons turned to look at him. On the surface his voice sounded even more casual, to the point of sarcasm. It emphasized rather than masked the tension that ran beneath.

"It's very simple. We will drive up, find out who these people are and have a little discussion about what's going on. If they decline to discuss the matter with me, I will counsel them to see the error of their ways." As an afterthought, he added, "Of course, that means we've gotta take them alive."

"Or at least one of them," Blancanales agreed.

"There it is!" Gadgets had interrupted when they drew up to 4557.

At that moment a heavyset man of about forty stepped out of the house. He had long red hair and a beard and wore dirty jeans with a Western shirt. The man started toward an old pickup truck parked on what had once been the lawn of the house.

Suddenly he saw the official-looking car approaching. Abruptly the man turned and ran back into the house.

"That's it!" Lyons said excitedly. He jerked the wheel sharply to the left and drove up onto the lawn, bailed out of the car and dashed after the retreating figure.

"Do it legally," part of him said as he got to the front door.

"Just do it," another part advised.

It was a decision he didn't have to make. Red Beard or somebody else inside made it for him.

The survival instinct reminded him not to stand directly in front of the door. Instead he approached off to one side.

A shotgun blast echoed inside the house. A panel of wood at about chest height exploded outward from the center of the old and cheap door. The pellets, double-ought buckshot from the way the door came apart, went by him. Splinters stung his arm and shoulder.

He was reminded of Hogan's arm.

Lyons snapped his fingers to Blancanales and Gadgets, then motioned them sharply around to back of the house, one in each direction. Then hugging the stucco to the left of the door, he rapped sharply on the intact wooden portion.

"Federal officers! Open up!"

Another blast hit the door, then a third.

Lyons sprang into action. To the left of the door, behind where Lyons stood, was a window. The space between the door and window was about four feet of stucco wall.

It was very simple. While Red Beard or whoever was inside was killing the door, he couldn't be aiming at the window. Hopefully.

Lyons whirled to his left.

Through the grimy glass he saw the man racking the action of a pump shotgun, getting ready to fire another load of buck at the door.

This time Lyons didn't talk. He didn't try to do it legally.

Three shots exploded from the Magnum. They came in such quick succession they might as well have been fully automatic.

All hit dead center. In less than a second the man's body absorbed some 1500 foot-pounds of energy from the high-velocity loads. The shotgun clattered to the floor as he staggered back against the wall.

Lyons didn't hesitate. He knew that when you're on the power curve you have to use the momentum, as though you were catching a big wave on a surfboard.

Once, a long time ago, he had talked to a race car driver about winning Formula races. "Go against your instincts," the guy had said. "Or maybe I've got that bass-ackwards. Maybe it's the conditioned responses you're going against, and you're actually going back to your instincts."

Lyons had listened, but the driver wasn't making any sense. The man was obviously a bit psycho. Why waste time talking to him.

Lyons had shrugged it off.

Seeing the Ironman's reaction, the racer had explained what he meant.

"When your mind says slow down, you've got to go faster. When somebody wipes out and fries his ass in 10,000 degrees of petroleum hi-tech, it makes you want to slow down. Right?"

Lyons nodded.

"Well, you shouldn't. That's when you've got to put your foot down and go for it."

Lyons had looked at the man with a new respect. Whatever else the guy was, he had guts. Crazy maybe, but brave. Of course, he had wiped out some of the finest race cars on the track, each time miraculously escaping from the hi-tech funeral pyre. But he also won his share of races.

Including his last one.

Only that hadn't been in a Formula One wheeled rocket. That had been in a piece-of-shit truck, loaded with a nuclear warhead. Instead of a LeMans, it had been the burning plains of Iran. The nuke was ticking down, and the crazy bastard had driven it away from his buddies and into the enemy camp, racing the clock, nursing every ounce of juice out of the old crate and winning with a half a second to spare.

Only thing was, he hadn't walked away from that one.

Lyons knew that someday he, too, was going to get into one that he wouldn't walk away from. Worrying about it didn't do any good, of course, but from time to time he wondered with a sort of detached curiosity if this was going to be the one....

In the meantime, Vince Biondi's words served him well, at least at times like this.

The brain's first reaction was to jump back to the cover of the stucco wall. Wait, assess the situation, see if the others inside would give it up with Red Beard out of the picture.

Also, reload, with three out of six gone.

That was what the mind said, all right.

Lyons ignored it and burst through the splintered door like the Schlitz malt-liquor bull. He held the Magnum in his right hand, muzzle up, back by the side of his shoulder, and led with his brawny left forearm. The already splintered door panels broke inward, the frame twisting behind him.

A couple of the empties from Red Beard's shotgun lay just inside the door on the tile floor. It was too late to change his course, and Lyons stepped directly on one of them as he prepared to dive into the room.

The casing rolled like a ball bearing. Instead of providing a push-off, his foot shot out backward, and the Ironman fell heavily on his belly, full-length on the dirty floor, and directly under the spray of automatic weapon fire that came from the hallway.

The gunman had anticipated that Lyons would make a diving entry and had acted accordingly. The burst went exactly where Lyons would have been if his move had come off as planned.

Slipping on the empty shotgun casing had saved his life. Even as this flashed through his mind, Lyons could sense the message was getting through to the man with the automatic weapon, and he would be shifting his spray downward.

Lyons twisted and fired. At the same instant, more gunfire blasted in the rear of the dwelling. It was the heavy authoritative boom of a .45 that punctuated the sharp chatter of the 9 mm three times. Down the hall behind his target, Lyons caught a glimpse of the man with the .45.

Blancanales.

The man with the automatic weapon arched backward. The muzzle of his gun drifted upward, blasting a line of bullet holes into the dirty plaster walls and ceiling. Then his grip on the trigger relaxed, and the firing stopped abruptly.

Lyons looked around him.

Nobody else. No sound in the ear-ringing aftermath of the close-quarters gunfire. It flashed through his mind that if they had killed everybody, there would be no leads to follow.

Then he heard sounds from the back of the house. Voices. People talking.

Blancanales. Gadgets.

And somebody else. A woman.

Lyons let out a sigh of relief. They had their lead.

14

The battered blue van cruised slowly past the house at 4557 Adams after Able Team had driven onto the lawn and bailed out.

The van continued to the end of the street then made a right turn. Less than a hundred feet later, it made another right so that it was coming back toward 4557.

The difference was that the road the van was now on was higher than Adams Avenue. A steep bank separated the two streets—so steep that there were no houses on that side of the higher road.

M.D. stopped the van above 4557. He killed the engine, crawled into the back and got out a pair of field glasses. He focused them and gazed down at the house below.

He knew the house, of course.

Red was a friend of Buffalo's. M.D. had run with both of them over the years.

But Buffalo was dead. Slimy and the others were dead, too.

M.D.'s job had been complete—as far as what Crank had asked him to do—the moment he had learned that. But when the Feds had run out, he knew there was more.

Same job, different subjects.

First the blond man had dashed into the house. Next he and his two companions, the older guy and the Mexican, had emerged. They'd had a hasty conference with the tall lean guy in charge, then the three of them had taken off in the car.

It didn't take a nuclear scientist to figure out they were on another scent.

M.D. reasoned that if Crank wanted any leaks at Branson's end plugged, he would probably want the same elsewhere.

Then, when they ended up going to Red's place, he was sure of it.

He put aside the glasses and took out his .30-06.

It was a lovely weapon, a Weatherby Vanguard. Bolt action, magazine capacity of five, plus one in the chamber. The highly polished factory luster of the stock and blueing had been carefully matted out, so that it was no longer shiny.

M.D. had mounted a scope on the rifle, a 3.5 to 10 power Leupold. The variable power allowed him to adjust for different range, terrain and lighting. The sight picture or reticle was a modified cross hair called a duplex, where the hairs became suddenly more fine or narrow just before they intersected. The effect was to make a sort of "sight-box" that focused on the major part of the target, but also had the fine-tuning of the hairs in the center.

No fancy red dots or laser lights for him. In these matters, M.D. saw himself as a traditionalist, a mountain man.

The ammunition was factory, Winchester/Western Silvertip, with a 180-grain bullet. From the 24-inch barrel on the Weatherby, the round came cooking out at a muzzle velocity of 2700 feet per second. The energy at a hundred yards was still something over 2400 foot-pounds. The specially designed hollowpoint round would peel back and mushroom on impact, making a surface of about half an inch.

Knockdown power. Virtually all the energy from the bullet would be transmitted to the target.

A solid hit would take down an elk. It should do the same or more to a person.

M.D. stroked the weapon lovingly.

The range was short, maybe 80 yards. Carefully he turned the Leupold down to minimum power. Then, putting the weapon aside, he again picked up the field glasses and settled down to wait.

He didn't have to wait long. There was a clear view through the front windows of the house. And now it was easy to tell what had transpired inside.

The Feds had killed Red and Mike. They had Red's old lady in the living room and were talking to her. And the bitch was answering. He could see it. She was talking her head off, just like Crank had known somebody would do.

Fuckin' women, he thought.

It was time to go into action. For Crank and the others. For the cause.

The window on the right side of his van, overlooking Red's place, was louvered.

M.D. dragged a small crate over and set it on end, making a perfect bench rest for the rifle.

M.D.'s back nearly touched the far wall of the van as he knelt on the floor. It was a perfect aiming position, the muzzle between the louvered panes of glass. His elbow was solid on the end of the wooden crate. It felt right.

He couldn't miss.

Gently he fed five rounds into the rifle's magazine. He pushed each cartridge down with the next, enjoying the feel of the weapon's precision. Then he closed the bolt and turned it downward.

Through the scope M.D. found the shattered door, then to the left the window. Then he had his target.

It would be real easy to take them all out, or at least a couple. But Crank was real clear on that—he wasn't after the Feds, just the girl, the traitorous bitch who could undo everything they were fighting for.

The Mex was kneeling in front of her. With the angle of her chair, that was no sweat. M.D. knew he could put one over the guy's shoulder. There was one problem, though. The big blond guy was standing in the way.

M.D. considered the ballistics.

He could probably shoot through the blond guy.

All he would have to do would be to deliberately aim below the chest. With the downward angle and the blond man standing and the girl sitting, he could put one into the man's back right below the ribs. If he did it right, there would be no bones to deflect the projectile. It would come out a little lower in front and still have enough juice to take the girl dead center in the chest.

Right between the tits, he thought.

If it'll knock down eight hundred pounds of elk, it'll take out these two enemies.

Excitement rushed through him. A smile spread over his face, and he nodded to himself.

It would be beautiful, one for the record books. Crank had said not the cops, but this was different. He wasn't trying to kill the Fed; he was killing the girl. The guy just happened to be in the way. If you can't go around 'em, you go through 'em.

Beautiful, beautiful, beautiful.

He snuggled his cheek against the stock.

The blond man suddenly turned and walked a couple of steps away.

Disappointment flooded M.D., but only for a second. Oh, well, no matter. The record would just have to wait. Crank would like this better, anyway. And Crank was the boss.

The cross hairs settled on target, and the gun fired itself at just the right moment.

THE GIRL STOOD with her head down. A high-frequency tremor shook her body.

Lyons regarded her grimly. Disgust rose in his throat. She can't be more than sixteen or seventeen, he thought. Yet she had the thin, soft, strung-too-tight pathos of the "meth monster."

She wore shorts and a dirty tank top. The top was made of a thin, white fabric. It sported the announcement Red's #1 Old Lady in red block letters stenciled unevenly on the back. Her nipples showed through the material as two dark circles on loose, pendulous breasts. Bruises, some fresh and some fading, made blue and saffron blotches on her legs.

Teenage baby fat had been rotted away by drugs and abuse.

Lyons took her chin gently in his hand and turned her face toward him. She complied without spirit. He scanned her face then her arms and legs with a practiced eye, noting the telltale signs.

The dark circles around the eyes and the hollowed cheeks told the story.

Methamphetamine. Crystal. "Crank" on the street.

He'd seen it a thousand times before. The crank was ridiculously easy to make. Anybody could cook it up in a garage, given a few ingredients. There were a few drawbacks, of course, one being the strong chemical odor that was a dead giveaway that the people inside were cooking something besides dinner.

Another drawback was that the makeshift labs frequently exploded. The chemicals were highly volatile, and any spark could set them off. When that happened, the results were spectacular—the blast would level the house and blow apart anybody inside.

But the profits were staggering. To the cookers, the dealers and the users, it was the "poor boy's cocaine." Even the relatively small peddlers, the ounce-level guys, could make a few thousand a month, tax free. The cookers and big dealers made ten or more times that much.

In California, as in many other areas, the majority of the meth market was controlled by outlaw motorcycle gangs or their associates.

They made it. They sold it. And they used it.

Instant energy. Crazy courage. Mondo strength. Major confidence. Around-the-clock go-power.

But the body only has so much in reserve, mentally or physically. Overdraw it too much, for too long, and psychosis sets in, along with hallucinations, malnutrition and physical collapse.

Idly Lyons wondered when this girl had eaten last and what it had been. A candy bar, probably, or french fries. And a line of crank.

He had seen it before in a thousand victims of this so-called "victimless crime." The waif who called herself Red's #1 Old Lady was just one more.

So why do you give a damn, Ironman, he asked himself. She doesn't, why should you?

Maybe I don't anymore, he thought. Then his gaze fell on the red that peppered his forearm.

Hogan.

That's why you care. For Hogan and Danny Williams and all the others, the good guys who fight the good fight for no better reason that it's the right thing to do.

"Well?" The girl's voice was as dead as her eyes.

"Well, what?" Lyons snarled.

"Well, go ahead. Do your thing."

"What do you mean?"

"You know. Arrest me. Read me my rights. Do your thing, pig." But the flat voice made the words more listless than hostile.

They were standing between the living room and the dining area of the small house. Lyons reached out with one foot and hooked a cheap metal kitchen chair. He dragged it over and pushed the girl down into it. He leaned forward so that his face was only a couple of inches away from hers.

At that distance he could smell the sour decay of her body, her hair, her breath.

"Listen to me, sweetheart, and listen good." His voice was harsh. "There's two dead guys in here. There's four more over at Buffalo's place, plus a couple of cops. And there's another stack of stiffs from that little armored car caper yesterday, so don't be givin' me that shit!"

He shouted the last word, his face nearly touching hers, focusing all his anger on her.

For a moment there was no reaction. Then her eyes widened slightly, and she turned toward him.

"Buffalo? Did you say Buffalo?"

"Right on, babe."

When she spoke again, her voice became soft and filled with wonderment like a child's. Lyons realized she was clicking in and out of touch with reality, slipping into a trancelike state. It was as if she were speaking to herself aloud rather than to them.

"He's dead. The Buff is dead, isn't he? I never thought he could die. He can't die. But he did. You killed him."

"That we did," said Lyons harshly.

"No, you didn't. You couldn't. Nobody could kill him. Buffalo and Crank—man, they're forever. You can't stop them. Nobody can."

"Forget the goddamn crank, lady. Leave that to the narcs. Tell us who Buffalo ran with."

She began singing in a soft, high voice, moving her thin body back and forth in time to the tune. It was a fairy tale, a little girl's song, sung by the little girl somewhere inside this juiced-out shell.

Ding, Dong, the Buff is dead,
the wicked Buff, the wicked Buff,
Ding, Dong, the wicked Buff is dead.

Lyons looked up at his partners. Gadgets gave a fatalistic shrug. Blancanales gazed at the waiflike form in pity. Then he moved Lyons to one side and knelt before the girl.

"What's your name, *niña*?" he asked, his voice soft.

"Huh?" She gave a start, as though his question came as an interruption to her trance.

"Your name, *niña*. What is it?" Sorrow clouded his brown eyes as his gentle voice probed the wreckage of the girl's psyche.

She looked sadly downward, a little girl who's been bad and is about to be punished. "Janice Lynn Freeman."

"Janice? Can I call you Janice?"

"Jan," she said, still looking down, with the timid firmness of a five-year-old. Then, with the defiance of someone much older, she added, "I'm Red's number-one old lady."

Blancanales decided to take a guess at a couple of things, hoping it would focus her attention.

"Jan." Pol's voice was barely above a whisper. "Red and Buffalo were friends. Some people came to see them. Who was it?"

"Nobody. Crank. Crank is king. The boss. All them guys and crank."

Blancanales shook his head. "I'm not talking about drugs, Jan. Forget about the crank. I'm asking you who it was."

But she wasn't responding. Her voice took on a trembling hysteria. Her neck and shoulders became rigid, and her head started to vibrate. She wasn't in the room anymore—she was somewhere else, at another time and place, getting a firsthand rerun of her own private hell.

"Crank's bad, man. Real bad. Crank'll hurt you. Fuck you up, all the way. Right up the ass. Crank fucked me right up the ass. And there ain't nothin' to do about it. Fuckin' no way."

Great sobs suddenly racked her body. She choked and shook, hugging her arms across her stomach and throwing her head from side to side. Then, as though a giant hand had grabbed her, she became still again.

"It's a beautiful place," she said in the little-girl voice. "All green, with plants and stuff. It's in the forest, way away from everybody."

"Where, Jan?"

"Up north. Way up north."

"Oregon? Washington?"

"No, silly." Again, the child was speaking. "In California. It's so beautiful. But it's also bad. Real bad. Crank's real bad."

The three men exchanged glances. It wasn't much, a crumb, really, but it was something.

"What's real bad, Jan?" asked Blancanales.

"Killing. Killing people. People that never did nothin' wrong, not really, anyways."

"Who does that, Jan?"

"Crank. Crank does that. I know. I seen it."

Lyons turned away disgustedly. For a moment it looked like she was going to give them something useful. But here she was, back to the dope stuff again.

He jammed his hands into his pockets and walked a few steps into the kitchen.

Glass shattered in the living room. At almost the same instant there came the unmistakable *whump* of a bullet hitting flesh. Only then, a slight but measurable pause later, did the sound of the gunshot reach their ears.

The questioning was over.

15

The girl's body spasmed backward. The chair tipped over, and she went with it.

Able Team reacted to survive.

Blancanales dived one way, Gadgets went the other. Lyons spun around and leaped toward the wall, out of sight of what he instantly saw as the source of the fire—the blue van parked on the next street above the rise.

"It's up there, up the bank!" Lyons shouted.

Blancanales and Gadgets, still in sight of the van through the window, scrambled for cover. They expected at any instant the next shots that would inevitably come before they got to safety.

None came.

Moments later the sound of the van's engine being started reached them.

"He's taking off!" shouted Gadgets.

Lyons looked back at the girl. She lay on her side, arms and legs sprawled in the peculiar bonelessness of the recently dead. Only God could do anything for her at this point.

"Let's go!" he snapped.

They sprinted for their car. Above them, the van had made it to the end of the street and was turning left, going out of sight.

For a frustrating moment the car's engine ground without catching. Then it roared to life. Dirt and gravel flew as the tires spun, making metallic clinks against the car's fenders and against the body of Red's nearby truck as they slewed across the lawn and onto the street.

Tires screeched as they slid broadside around the corner. Above them, the street was empty. Lyons jammed his foot to the floor, and the car leaped forward.

They crested the rise in time to see the van make a screeching left turn onto another street. A paperboy was negotiating his bicycle from the sidewalk down into the street. The van skidded sideways, fighting the momentum of its earlier path and struggling to make the turn. The rear corner panel smacked into the boy, knocking him and his papers and bike into a tangled heap on the sidewalk.

"I'll kill that bastard!" said Blancanales between clenched teeth.

"Not before we talk to him," Lyons retorted. "He's our last chance to pick up the trail."

They skidded around the same corner. The paperboy looked unharmed, but his pale face was streaked with tears. His bicycle was twisted and mangled beyond repair. Newspapers littered the sidewalk and gutter.

Lyons made a silent promise to set things right with the kid when all this was over.

Ahead of them the van turned sharply onto the freeway on-ramp. Even at six-thirty in the morning, a line of cars waited. The van swerved to miss them but didn't make it. It clipped the last one in line, a yellow VW, sending it crashing into the car ahead of it. Glass shattered and metal crunched.

"He'll never make it," Blancanales predicted. "We've got him now."

For a moment it looked as though the Politician was right. The van swerved crazily but somehow straightened out and shot past the line of waiting cars onto the freeway.

Lyons remembered the advice of Vince Biondi, the race car driver, and put his foot down harder. The sedan roared past the line of motorists.

The freeway traffic was building up, but it was still fast. The van swerved in and out between the morning commuters, with Able Team's sedan in hot pursuit.

And closing the gap. Then, abruptly, the van swerved to take an off-ramp two lanes away to the right. Tires screeched and horns blared as the killer cut across traffic. Able Team stayed with it.

The two vehicles almost made it.

The van was just a split second too late to make the slicing angle of the off-ramp. With a scream of smoking tire rubber, it skidded left. It hit the raised concrete berm and flipped over. The off-ramp was built onto a long, downhill slope, planted with thick, pulpy ice plant. The van rolled sideways down the embankment.

"Geronimo!"

Lyons shouted it at the top of his lungs as they followed the van. A deafening crash shook the car as the front undercarriage hit the curb. The men inside were hurled forward, and then the car was over the berm and plunging headfirst down the embankment after the van.

"Go for it!" Gadgets shouted from the back seat.

They didn't have any choice. Lyons spun the steering wheel, trying to steer the car to where the van had rolled. The sedan slid crazily on the slippery plant juice from the ground cover. Then he started to lose it. The rear of the car began to come around, putting them into the beginnings of a sideways slide—a "side-slide," as they used to call it on the PD.

The side-slide became a broadside.

Lyons could see the van had come to a stop below them.

It lay on its side, the roof facing uphill. Amazingly, the driver was scrambling out, apparently unhurt; maybe he was trying to get out fast in case the gasoline ignited. He levered his body up through the shattered window like a gymnast, swinging himself around to drop to the ground on the uphill side.

The side Able Team was sliding toward.

With a terrible slow-motion understanding, Lyons realized the inevitable outcome.

The sedan was nearly broadside now. The tires useless for steering, it skidded sideways down the slope at thirty or forty miles an hour, bearing down on the van. Their quarry dropped to the ground. He landed in a crouch and started to rise to his feet, just in time for the two vehicles to come together with a broadside-to-roofside crash.

It was a biker terrorist sandwich, rare, pressed extra thin.

The man's head was just at the height of the open window next to Blancanales, the right front side. His body was between the sedan's door and the van's top.

Above the crash of the metal, there was a sound like a wet splat. It was combined with the hard crackle of ribs compressing then breaking. The killer's eyes bulged from the hydrostatic pressure from below. A gout of blood and stomach fluids shot from his mouth and nose. Then his head lolled forward into the sedan.

Suddenly it was very quiet. The only sound inside the car was a steady spatter as the blood that streamed from the killer's mouth hit and pooled in the passenger footwell of the sedan.

Lyons shook his head to clear it then tried his door. It didn't move. He heaved his body against it, and it popped open, dumping him onto the dirt and bruised ice plant. He leaned over and dragged the semiconscious Politician out then extended his hand to Gadgets. The smell of raw gasoline permeated the air.

The three of them scrambled to safety.

The upended van's gasoline tank was dripping steadily, and the fuel pooled in a recess in the undercarriage. When the hollow was filled, it ran down the chassis until it hit the hot muffler.

With a flash and a *whoomp!* the van exploded. Battered and bruised, the men of Able Team mutely sat on the ice plant and watched as their last link to the killers went from rare to medium to extra crispy.

16

It was just past ten o'clock that night when Lyons found her house. He pulled the rented Chevy Citation to the curb and killed the engine.

It was autopilot all the way.

Fatigue numbed his brain. A goose-egg size bruise above his left ear throbbed with every beat of his heart. He knew he should have been back at the motel with Blancanales and Gadgets. But something—he didn't know what—drew him to her house.

He had had better days. This one certainly was not even in the running for okay, let alone good.

The last chance at a lead to their target died before their very eyes. Extreme close-up, in fact—zoom lens, slow-mo, instant replay available. The killer had been first squashed and then cooked. They had gazed on helplessly as the trail went up in smoke.

"*Madre de Dios,*" Blancanales had observed with a sigh. "Now what, amigos?"

Gadgets shook his head, for once at a loss for words.

Lyons, however, had been beside himself with fury.

"Who *are* these guys?" he exploded between clenched teeth, the cords on his neck standing up from the tension. "They're killing cops. They're operating right under our very noses. And when we go after them, they're kicking our asses at every turn!"

Nobody responded.

Lyons pushed himself to his feet and began walking in a small circle. Then he stopped and looked over at his partners.

"These guys are worse than the fucking Russians," he railed. "We start to get close, and the door slams in our faces. Every time we might get a lead, somebody gets dead. Then we get another chance, and that guy gets dead, too. And here we are—we end up following a trail of bodies!"

The other two knew there was no point in trying to reason with him when he was in this state. They'd seen it before. It was just a part of Carl Lyons—a part of his strength, a part of his weakness.

"Well," observed Gadgets with a wink at Blancanales, "we won't have to worry about it for a while, anyway."

"What do you mean?" Lyons demanded.

"This isn't Central America, it's central L.A. We can't just leave 'em where they fall. We can't even let somebody else do the clean-up. We're federal agents, remember? As of yesterday. I have a hunch we're going to be busy with red tape."

Lyons digested that. Then, oddly, it seemed to break the tension, and he grinned ruefully. Then he laughed out loud.

"You think they're going to make us pick up our own bodies?" he asked facetiously.

"There's a good chance."

"Probably a ton of paperwork for each stiff, too," added Blancanales.

Lyons emitted a stage groan.

"Probably have to be on the right forms. In triplicate, too," the Politician continued.

"And if it's not right, they'll bounce it right back to you," added Gadgets.

"Probably won't even get paid until it's done, either," rejoined Blancanales.

Lyons groaned even louder.

"Look, buddy," the Politician continued in mock disapproval, pushing the charade to the max, "nobody said it was going to be a bed of roses. You play, you pay. You can't just do the fun stuff and leave the paperwork to somebody else. It's every man for himself."

"Some friends," muttered Lyons.

"Hey. It's a jungle out there."

The jiving predictions hadn't been wrong. Even with the aid of Chandler and the Major Disaster Team, the debriefing and recording had been a bureaucratic nightmare. It was after eight that night before they could get away, and then only on a dozen promises to "get right on" several things first thing in the morning.

They were promises that Lyons, for one, had no intention of keeping, as he informed the others later on.

Gadgets professed to be shocked. "You mean, you lied to them?"

Lyons shook his head. "No. I didn't lie to them. I bullshitted them a little, that's all."

"What's the difference?"

"If you have to ask, you wouldn't understand the answer."

Gadgets wrinkled his brow. "Now, *that's* a bullshit answer if I ever heard one."

"Police department training," suggested Blancanales in agreement.

They had made their escape and chowed down a listless meal at a nearby Denny's, then headed for a motel. By then the postcombat adrenaline was long gone. Fatigue combined with emotional letdown to produce a mind-numbing haze.

Lyons had taken a shower then suddenly announced he had somewhere to go. The others hadn't been able to change his mind, and now he was standing outside Margaret's town house in La Crescenta, just above Glendale and near his own home town of Montrose.

He wondered if she would still be up at this hour. The glow of lights through the curtain provided the answer. Then it occurred to him that he didn't even know if she was tied down or had a roommate, man or woman.

He hesitated, but only for a moment.

To hell with it. If there was a boyfriend, and he didn't like it, tough. Lyons would reason with him. And if that didn't work . . .

Besides, he wasn't going there for romantic purposes. It was for—he realized he didn't know why he was going there. There was something he had to find out, something that was drawing him there, but he didn't know what it was. He also didn't know what to expect in the way of a welcome.

His fears were groundless. At the soft, two-toned bong, the door opened immediately. She was wearing khaki shorts and a red top, both of which did great things for her tan and her short brown hair.

"Hello, Carl." She didn't seemed surprised. Or hostile.

He suddenly felt clumsy, unsure of himself. "Hi, Marge."

They stood for a moment, then she gave a little smile. "Would you like to come in?"

He nodded, and she led the way.

Inside the decor was an elegant range of browns and grays. The distinctive odor of decorator-dried plants hung in the air. She waved him to a chair then sat on the couch herself, tucking her legs under her.

Lyons couldn't help noticing they were still damn fine legs.

"Nice place." What the hell, he thought, it was something to say, at least.

"Thank you." She paused. "I was wondering if you'd come around, or call."

"Yeah. Me, too. But here I am."

"Why did you want to see me?"

He thought about that for a moment. "I don't really know, I guess. Why did you wonder if I would?"

She got suddenly off the couch and walked to the window. The front of the town house faced southwest, overlooking a blanket of city lights. She gazed out for a long time without speaking.

"It's not easy, is it?"

Lyons wondered what she meant—seeing him, talking about it, being an adult, or what? He let the silence ride.

"We think we have all the answers when we're young, don't we? All that is necessary is to tell other people about them. Only then you get out on your own, and suddenly you don't have any of the answers."

Lyons could relate to that. "I know what you mean."

She went on as though he hadn't spoken. "And I'm supposed to help people. Help them understand themselves." She gave a short, humorless laugh. "I can't even understand myself."

Lyons didn't respond.

"And you," she said, "you always had all the answers. Whatever needed doing, you were the guy to do it. Nothing stopped you. Nothing got to you."

"Don't bet on it."

"That's why I was so—" she fumbled for the word "—so unreasonable about those guys that attacked us. Even though I knew you were right."

Her voice was shaky. Lyons got to his feet and stood behind her. He put his hands uncertainly on her shoulders. She stood for a moment then turned to face him. Her eyes searched his face.

"Does anything get to you now, Carl?"

Unconsciously, his gaze dropped to the arm where Hogan's blood had been. A lot of good ones had died, along with a lot more of the bad ones. Were they making progress? Did it matter? He felt strangely unmoved, as if he were losing the ability to feel anything. It scared him a little.

He looked back at her face. "Not much."

"Do you still have all the answers?"

He started to say that he never had. Instead he replied simply, "No."

She reached up and touched his cheek. It was all he could do not to flinch. Then she moved her fingertips to the creases at the corner of his eyes. "You're hurting, aren't you?"

"I don't honestly know." Christ, he thought, what's the matter with me?

Then she was in his arms, pulling his face down to hers. He felt her lips on his forehead and on his eyes, touching him with a tenderness so exquisite that he had a momentary fear he might cry.

The surge of emotion released the tension that held him so tightly in check. Urgency replaced uncertainty, and he kissed her hungrily. Their tongues met, touched and explored each other with a shared need. He put his arms around her, and she molded herself to him, pressing herself against his groin, then shifting to one side so that his leg fit between hers. He felt her fingers knead the back of his neck, then trace a line with one fingernail down the trapezius muscle that ran to his shoulder.

They broke the kiss, and he moved his lips to the hollow of her neck. His tongue tasted her skin and sensed the downlike hair. Suddenly she gave a little gasp, and melted against him. Her head lolled to one side, offering the spot on her neck to his lips.

Her hands slipped from his neck to the center of his back. She ran her fingers in the groove along his spine then pressed the thick cords of muscle on either side, touching, feeling, exploring. His groin ached, and he pushed artlessly toward her. With his hands he stroked her back then raised the back of her shirt so he could feel the silkiness beneath it.

He felt her give a slight shudder. He stepped back a half step, separating them, so he could lift her shirt and slide it upward. Her arms raised without protest, and he slipped it up and over her head.

She gave a single combing push to her short brown hair with one hand then stepped toward him again. She was not wearing a bra, and the white skin of her breasts in contrast to the darker tan above and below somehow made her look even more naked. He lightly stroked her sides, then the sides of her breasts, then grazed the nipples with the rough hardness of his hands. She made a little gasping sound then urgently began to unbutton his shirt.

He put an arm around her shoulders and another behind her legs and lifted her easily. He thought about taking her into the bedroom then said to hell with it and knelt on the carpet to lay her gently down on her back. His hands found the khaki shorts, and she lifted first her buttocks and then her legs to help him. Her panties were pale blue and delicate against the brown skin, overlying the hint of soft darkness between her legs.

They kissed hungrily then he moved downward—neck, breasts, belly, and then to the exquisite womanness below. He nuzzled her above the panties then slid them down and touched her, teased her, caressed her with his tongue. She moaned and lifted herself to him. Hastily he shed the rest of his clothing and moved up to join her in the timeless affirmation of feeling, of sensation, of pleasure, of life itself.

"WHEW!" She gave a long, shaky sigh.

He grinned. "Funny, I was just thinking the same thing."

Lyons lay on his back on the thick carpet, one forearm under his head. Margaret lay on her side, next to him, her head braced on the palm of one hand. She traced little circles on his chest with one finger.

"You know," she said, "I was carrying a ton of 'uptightness,' especially since Danny died. And that got rid of it all."

"Is that the psychological term? 'Uptightness?' "

"Not exactly. And this isn't the recommended treatment, either."

He winked. "It worked, didn't it? But just because you're starting to feel better doesn't mean you should discontinue the treatments. It's important to, uh, take the whole series, you know?"

She smiled, but her next words were serious. "The worst thing about his death was that I really didn't feel anything. Not at first, anyway. It scared me. I think that's part of why I was so rotten to you."

"Forget it."

"He was really a good kid, you know," she said fondly.

"I know."

"And I know this sounds crazy, after that little scene in the hospital garage, but I hope you get the guys who killed him."

Lyons turned and gave her a searching look.

"I mean it. And I know it won't bring him back, and all that stuff. But it's wrong that he died that way—well, that all of them did—and they ought to pay."

"Good girl." Lyons deliberately kept his voice casual. "I had the same idea myself, and I'm all fired up to do it. Only problem is, I don't have the faintest idea who it is I should be getting."

She looked at him. "What about all that business today? Didn't that—"

"That got us nowhere."

She fell silent then spoke again. "Danny said something at the hospital. It was right after they brought him out of surgery. He was conscious, semi, anyway, for a while. He kept trying to say these two words."

Lyons turned his head to look at her. "So tell me."

She sat up, beautiful and naked in the soft light. "I'm trying to remember. It didn't make much sense. One of them was 'crank,' I think. Yes, that's it, 'crank.' And 'crazzy.' Like 'jazzy,' only with a *cr*. He kept trying to say it, over and over—'crank crazzy, crank crazzy.' Then he—" her voice trembled and she swallowed hard "—then he lost consciousness. That was right before you got there."

Lyons sat bolt upright. "Are you sure those were the words?" he inquired urgently.

She nodded. "I think so. No, I'm sure. That was it. I didn't tell you at the time because it didn't make any sense, and because I was mad. Then I forgot it, I guess. Is it important?"

Lyons was still there, but he was a million miles away. His mind was racing, scanning back to what that juiced-out girl had said before she took the ought-six bullet in the sternum.

"Crank." Crank that was so bad. Crank that hurt you. Crank that killed people.

And now a dead man was telling him the same thing. Danny Williams, good man and a good cop that he had been, was giving him the message that maybe Red's number one old lady wasn't talking about drugs at all.

"Crank" was a name.

That had to be it. And the other word, the one that sounded like "crazzy." Maybe that was the dude's last name, or something close to it. Cassie, maybe? Krasner? Krasne?

Stony Man's computers were cross-indexed phonetically. "The Bear" could ask them for "sound-alikes."

Lyons glanced at his watch then realized he'd taken it off sometime during the evening's festivities. Stark naked, he got to his feet and looked for a clock.

Twelve-thirty in the morning. That made it 3:30 A.M. back at Stony Man.

No sweat. "Early to rise" would be good for them back there.

Still naked, he walked to the telephone. Maybe it was darkest before the dawn, after all.

17

If a single word had to be chosen to describe Aaron "the Bear" Kurtzman, it would be "rumpled."

Rumpled, as in a bed whose covers were just pulled up without actually being made up.

Rumpled, as in that vaguely disorganized, baggy-tweed look of the true academic, the kindly, ivory-tower university professor with more degrees than a thermometer and an IQ higher than the national debt.

Rumpled, as in somebody who gets dragged out of his bed at 0330 hours by that psycho-maniac Carl Lyons, now out in California, who's got something that can't wait three hours.

The Bear scrubbed the sleep from his eyes with one hairy paw. Then, with a grumble that was half feigned, half real, he spoke into the receiver.

"Do you know what time it is?"

"Going on one o'clock here, guy. Makes it almost four where you are. Time to rise and shine."

Even routed and rerouted, checked and back-checked, and scrambled and unscrambled—all of which were mandatory in a secret call from a noncleared location—Lyons's voice sounded disgustingly cheerful, Kurtzman thought sourly. Bastard sounds like he just got laid. Or is just about to. Maybe both.

Lyons's voice spoke again.

"I need a trace."

"So what's new?"

"It's a name. It's our best lead so far. In fact, it just could be jackpot time."

Kurtzman reached for a yellow pad he kept on a clipboard next to the bed. A Mickey Mouse pencil was attached to the board by a string, one end of which was tied crudely around the pencil, while the other was tied to the spring clip. When any accurate measurement of your IQ—assuming one could be made—would be a three-digit number beginning with a "2," you didn't have to stand on ceremony or dignified props to be respected.

"Give me all the identifying information on your subject."

"Crank."

"What?"

"Crank. C-r-a-n-k. Crank. You know, like when you turn something. Crank."

Kurtzman wrote it down. "Okay, what's the last name?"

"I don't know."

There was a long pause. "You don't know."

"No. All I have is a sound-alike."

"Well, what is it?"

Lyons went through the "crazy-that-rhymes-with-jazzy" routine. When he was done, the Bear spoke again.

"DOB?"

"What?" came the voice from L.A.

"DOB. You know, date of birth. The guy's birthday. What is it?"

"I don't know."

"Physical? What does he look like?"

"I don't have that, either."

Kurtzman barked out a laugh. He was awake now, and he was getting intrigued. Despite the hard time he was giving

Lyons, the Bear thrived on intelligence requests such as this. He was a computer genius, whose compendious mind knew both the hardware—the electronics and mechanics involved in building the machines—and the software.

He could speak every programming language ever devised.

It was Kurtzman who was in charge of the voluminous data in the Stony Man data banks. "In charge of" meant compiling, sorting, analyzing and storing. In recent months, however, it had taken on a new meaning, as well.

Accessing.

Under his personal guidance, the Bear's computers became expert at tapping into networks and systems all over the world. Usually, those in charge of the "tappee" didn't even know it had occurred. Government, industrial, educational and communications networks—virtually none of them were safe. Kurtzman cracked security codes the way other people did crossword puzzles.

And now Lyons's problem intrigued him.

All he had were two words, presumably names, though they could be acronyms or code words. It wasn't much, but at least what there was was relatively unique, uncommon.

Still, it would simplify the task if he knew everything, however little it might be, about the two words he was being asked to trace. At least it would help in knowing what systems he should start with, and in discarding some of the possible answers.

"All right," he said to Lyons, "now tell me everything you can on this situation."

Lyons did. The Bear listened attentively, making occasional notes with Mickey Mouse. When Lyons finished, Kurtzman asked one final question.

"When do you need this?" He knew what the answer would be, of course, and he wasn't disappointed.

"Yesterday."
"Why did I ask?"
"What can I say?"

WRAPPED IN A HEAVY but tattered bathrobe, the Bear sat
before the console of Stony Man's boss computer. Before he
set finger to keyboard, though, he ran it through his own
mental computer.

Item: Assume it's a name. The dead cop either heard one
of his attackers say it or he recognized the person. Either
way, California is the place to start. Reaching for the yellow pad and clipboard, he jotted "name" and "CA."

Item: It's probably, though not certainly, a man's name.
While women are happy to get involved in terrorist shoot-
outs these days, there are still more men, so statistically,
that's probably right. Also, the name "Crank" just doesn't
sound like one a woman would use.

So let's assign a probability of point eight that it's a man's
name. He scribbled "male, .8" with the "mouse."

Now, about the second word, or name—that's got to be
the last name, while "crank" is the first name, or, more
likely, a nickname. He wrote "Crazzy (phonetic)—sur-
name, .9."

Item: Based on what Lyons had said, there was a pretty
fair chance the guy was either a member of an outlaw biker
gang or a drug dealer, the drug being methamphetamine.
Moreover, the guy would probably have an affinity for
firearms.

He wrote "biker, .3"; "dope dealer, .3"; and "gun vio-
lations, .2."

All of this meant something else, as well—the subject was
probably Caucasian—in California, meth was chiefly,
though not exclusively, a white boy's vice, and the over-
whelming majority of outlaw biker types were white, as well.

He wrote "WMA, .9" to indicate the probability the subject was a white male adult.

Lastly, he thought of the condition of the young cop, Danny Williams, when he had spoken the words. Assume you had been shot to shit then operated on and pumped full of drugs. You probably know you won't make it, so you try to say the name. But your mouth is like cotton wool, and the best you can do is something between a croak and a whisper.

Something that sounded like "crazzy-that-rhymes-with-jazzy."

The Bear spoke aloud, although only he and the computers were in the empty room. "All right, Aaron, me boy. Assuming all that, what sounds would you probably not be able to make? And what letters go with them? And lastly, which ones make a name if you add them to something that sounds like 'crazzy?' "

After a few moments he nodded to himself. A smile traced his lips.

He removed the top sheet of paper from the clipboard then wrote his best estimate of what the name would be and what characteristics the man would have. He then folded the paper and put it into an envelope and sealed it.

It was a game he played. See if you can beat the computer. Man versus machine. John Henry against the steam drill.

Then, and only then, did he key into the machine.

In about forty minutes he had the answer. And, apart from the specific details such as the man's height, weight, birthday, and criminal record, he'd been right on. So close, in fact, that he could count it as a victory—man over the machine.

It had really been too easy. He'd make sure he told Lyons that.

He reached for the telephone. Hopefully, the guy's asleep, Kurtzman thought, and it'll be my turn to wake him up.

"I'M SORRY, but I don't know how to make it do that."

The person who spoke was a pleasant young woman named Mary Peralta. She stood at the main console in the FBI's computer room in the Federal building in Los Angeles.

"What do you mean?" Lyons looked incredulous. Though he would have to count the preceding night as one of his best, an all-time high after an all-time low, between one thing and another he hadn't gotten much sleep. And now he was anxious to get the hard copy or printout of what the Bear had summarized to him over the phone.

Mary looked helpless. "I'm just filling in for Joyce, the regular compspec."

"The what?"

"Oh, sorry, computer specialist. She's the regular one. I'm just a trainee."

"Well, where is she? When will she be back?"

"Tomorrow. She's out sick."

Lyons rolled his eyes and turned away in disgust. He had to admit it wasn't right to be angry at either Mary or the FBI. Normally the Bureau was a model of efficiency in things like this. It's just that he was used to Stony Man, where things always got done *now*.

Blancanales spoke up, turning on the charm that led to his nickname. "Is there anybody else who might know?"

Mary thought it over. "Well, this is an unusual format, you see. Most of our stuff can be controlled completely by the sender, so it wouldn't make any difference once I keyed in the ID code at this end. But this isn't like that."

"Anybody?" Blancanales persisted.

"Well, there's a girl who works for the U.S. courts here in the building. She does a lot of their computer work. She might know."

"Can we get her up here?"

"I'll see."

Ten minutes later Mary returned with an attractive young woman in tow. "This is Tami Bonner," she said.

Blancanales cast an appreciative eye on the newcomer. Not great, he thought, but damn good. Now, if she's competent . . .

She wasn't. Or at least, she wasn't able to push the right buttons to make the connection. Ten more minutes went by, and they were still in the same place. Gadgets shot a glance at Lyons.

The Ironman wasn't saying anything, but his look could kill.

There was a knock on the door. Lyons opened it. A lanky youth of about seventeen stood there. He had red hair and freckles, a real all-American kid.

He looked past Lyons for Mary. She looked up, "Oh, hi, Eliot. What's up?"

"I heard you might need some help on getting an access to work," the youth said.

"Hell, come on in," said Lyons. He started to say something about going down to the street to round up a few winos and drag them in to see if maybe one of them might know how to do it, but he didn't.

Which was just as well. In about forty seconds the kid had the machine clicking and whirring happily away. It went through a series of identifying and security codes then began to print out the Bear's material.

"Anything else?" the young man inquired.

"Yes," said Lyons. "Who are you?" His manner was unintentionally brusque.

Mary Peralta answered. "This is Eliot Keir. He's working on a special project here through UCLA. It's sponsored by the Justice Department. And don't worry, he's cleared."

Lyons grinned and stuck out his hand. "I never doubted it," he said. "I just wanted to know who I was thanking. Thanks. I owe you one."

The youth smiled, mumbled something and departed. The others turned back to the printer.

After a page of the all-caps output, Tami said brightly, "Well, I have to be going, too, you guys. Sorry I wasn't able to be more help."

Blancanales smiled. "Thanks for your efforts. You, too, Mary."

The two women left. The Able Team men turned back to the printer. It whirred and clicked as the print mechanism flew back and forth on the continuous-feed computer paper, transmitting the information at last.

Three floors below them, Tami Bonner went into her office. She didn't bother to shut the door.

She picked up the telephone and punched 9 to get an outside line.

What luck, she thought in wonder. What total, mind-blowing, luck.

Good luck for Crank. Bad luck for the guys up in the FBI's computer room.

18

"If this is the guy, he is one hard-core, made-to-order dirt-bag, a heavy duty model," observed Blancanales.

"A formidable opponent," agreed Gadgets.

"It's the guy, all right," said Lyons grimly. "Those guys in the armored truck, and the cops, never had a chance."

They had their target, thanks to the Bear's uncanny genius and Stony Man's computers.

The printer in the FBI computer room had given them a hard copy of the stuff Kurtzman had compiled the past few hours.

It was impressive, to say the least. Moreover, it fit.

They scanned the first sheet, a biographical summary of the most important details.

STONYMAN TO ABLE
20 APR 86
CODEBLUE//EYES ONLY//FBI TRANS

DATASUM//BIO//
YOUR SUBJ. KRASNE, CARL ROBERT, DOB 10
OCT 44
  AKA CARL ROBERTS
  AKA BILL ROZETTI

N/N CRANK
N/N BC (POSSIBLY DER FROM BIG CARL)

N/N MAD DOG
N/N KILLER

PHYS.DATA
  WMA
  6'0''
  240
  HAIR/BRO
  EYE/BRO
  BLD/HVY MUSCULAR
  MARKS/SCARS/TATTOOS//SKULL W/ SNAKES,
  LFT.ARM//EAGLE W/ DRAGON, RT.ARM//
  WOMAN FACE, LFT.SHLDR.REAR//BORN TO
  KICK ASS, RT.SHLDER.REAR

CRIM.RECORD//REV.CHRONO

78// PRES	NO ENTRIES
74//78	CA DEPT CORRECTIONS, FOLSOM, MANSLAUGHTER, 2X, SENTENCE CONCURRENT, PAROLED MENDOCINO COUNTY//CO-DEFT. BRANSON, KENNETH NMN, DOB 06/06/49
76	ARR. MURDER IN PENAL INST., NO PROS
74	ARR. ASSAULT OFFICER DEADLY WEAPON, NOT GUILTY
74	ARR. ASSAULT PERSON DEADLY WEAPON., NO PROS, VICTIM NOT AVAIL.
72	ARR. RAPE, FORCED ORAL COPULATION, RESIST ARREST, CONV. RESIST ARREST, BALANCE NO PROS, VICTIM DECLINES/NOT AVAIL.

71	ARR. TRANSP. CONTROLLED SUBST, NOT GUILTY, EVIDENCE SUPPRESSED//IMPROPER SEARCH/SEIZURE
70	ARR. WIT. INTIMIDATION, FOUND NOT GUILTY, VICTIM NOT AVAIL.
66//69	CA DEPT CORRECTIONS, SOLEDAD, RAPE, PAROLED LOS ANGELES.
68	ARR. CONSPIRACY AND POSSESS. AUTO. WPN., NOT GUILTY EVIDENCE SUPPRESSED//IMPROPER SEARCH/SEIZURE
67	ARR. MURDER, NO PROS, INSUFF. EV.
65	ARR. POSSESS CONTROLLED SUBST. FOR SALE, PROBATION 3 YRS.
53//64	DETAIL NOT AVAIL; SEALED ORDER JUVENILE COURT, LOS ANGELES.

"That has to be our boy," observed Gadgets, pointing to the reference to Buffalo Branson.

Lyons nodded. "And check the record. It's a classic profile—a lot of arrests, damn few convictions, and even less hard time. And the times he gets arrested are only the tip of the iceberg."

"Also a lot of 'turn 'em loose' by the courts," said Gadgets, pointing to the "evidence suppressed" entries.

Lyons's jaw tightened. "That's the California Supreme Court for you. Rosie and the Reversals. Rose Bird and her cohorts. Biggest bunch of liberal jerk-offs in the nation."

The computer continued to whir, zipping out the data on associates, prison gang affiliation, modus operandi of some of his cases, and a psychological profile compiled while he was in prison. Also, thankfully, his last known address—a rural box number in Mendocino County in northern California.

Blancanales pointed to it. "Remember what the girl said, amigos? 'In the forest, all green, with plants and stuff,' something like that?"

Gadgets nodded. "It fits. What do you think, Ironman?"

Lyons was leaning back in an old metal steno chair in the computer room, arms folded across his chest. He appeared deep in thought. He responded without looking up.

"I think it's jackpot time, at last. And time to talk to the mother superior to find out our marching orders."

"I thought we had them," Blancanales countered. "Work with Chandler, do it legally, and maybe settle a few accounts along the way."

"Yeah, that's what it was, all right," Lyons continued.

"So what's changed?"

"Who knows? Me, for one, but I realize that doesn't count. If Krasne is the guy—and we know it is—the time for legal niceties is over. His account is way overdrawn. A more direct approach seems indicated."

Blancanales considered it. "Sounds okay to me."

"Got any suggestions?" asked Gadgets.

"Well, as a matter of fact, I do." Lyons looked up at them at last. His blue eyes were pale and cold. He gave a thin smile; it, too, had all the warmth of dry ice. He continued.

"We tried it the Supreme Court way. We gave it a hell of a try, in fact. And all we got was a bunch of dead folk, good guys and bad guys."

"Go on," said Blancanales.

"Now, Plan One having failed, it's time to fall back to Plan Two."

"And that is?"

"Simple. I think you'll like it. We fall back and kill the bastards."

They thought about it in silence. Then Blancanales nodded, stating the obvious in mock seriousness. "You're right. I like it."

"Me, too," said Gadgets.

Lyons smiled the icy smile again. "I thought you might."

19

"We in a hurry?"

The question came from Mike Chandler as he scanned the breakfast menu.

Lyons shook his head. "Take all the time you want. You might want to eat light, though."

Lyons turned to the waitress and ordered six eggs, over easy, a breakfast steak (rare), orange juice, a short stack of buttermilk hotcakes and coffee.

The waitress gaped. "Is this for all of you, or what?"

Blancanales nudged Chandler. "Keep an eye on Lyons. It looks like he's off his feed a little. If this keeps up, we'll have to take him to a vet for a vitamin shot."

"Nah," interposed Gadgets. "You heard him. He's eating light on purpose."

Chandler blinked. "And here I was wondering if we had time for me to order bacon and two eggs," he muttered.

L.A. was some four hundred miles behind them. The Strike Force and all its bureaucratic trappings were history for all of them, including Mike Chandler.

All things considered, it had been remarkably easy to arrange.

Lyons had called Brognola with his Plan Two. The head Fed had immediately approved of it, lock, stock and barrel. He had even suggested Mike Chandler should go along—good evidence that the Stony Man chief thought highly of the prosecutor.

"Is this going to have any impact on his career?" inquired Lyons. "Realizing I don't have a need to know, of course."

"Don't worry about his career. It's in good shape."

"Even after that business yesterday?"

Lyons had been concerned about the shoot-outs and the resulting lack of live bodies to prosecute. It wouldn't affect Able Team, of course—they were members of the Strike Force in name only, and even that was only temporary. As a result, they couldn't care less about the Justice Department's investigative stats. But Chandler was in a different boat; the Strike Force should be a special honor for his career.

"Especially after that. The folks who really know what's going on aren't the least bit displeased."

"Great." It didn't really make sense, but Lyons had shrugged and accepted it.

Brognola must have pulled some other strings as well; at least, that's what Lyons originally thought. For instance, the FBI had somehow mysteriously produced a van for Able Team to take up north with them—no questions asked. Moreover, the van turned out to contain weaponry, body armor and ammunition. There was even extra gear in it for Chandler.

It was only then that Lyons had understood—Brognola had been planning for this all along.

The van and equipment had undoubtedly been assembled at Brognola's direction. That direction had come well before Able Team was pulled into the caper. Lyons recalled that Blancanales had been in L.A. and had already been activated when the armored truck hijacking occurred.

The only logical conclusion was that Brognola had been planning a mission aimed at Group 504 all along. The hijacking just stepped up the timetable a little. Also, as originally planned, it was undoubtedly a "search and destroy" effort, because that was how Able Team operated. Somehow, for political reasons perhaps, Brognola had been forced to combine the team with the Strike Force, but it wouldn't have been his first choice.

But things have changed. Whatever had been the problem before, it was gone.

Now that things had gone to hell with doing it "the Supreme Court way," as Lyons had called it, Brognola could have Able Team do it their way.

Search and destroy. Fall back and kill.

Of course, the Stony Man operations chief had probably hoped they could, in fact, "do it legally." That probably would have suited him fine. But it was strictly secondary to the main mission, which was to find out who was behind the White Knights—Group 504—and take them out, using whatever means it took to get the job done.

And now that Brognola was convinced that Krasne was the target, he had spared nothing to locate him.

The results were impressive. By noon the Stony Man crew had pinpointed Krasne's base of operation.

It was a section, 640 acres, or a mile square, in the heart of the northern California wine and marijuana country. The land lay next to National Forest land. The deed said it was held in trust by the Church of the White Knights.

The location was a perfect choice for Krasne's organization.

For one thing, it was remote and inaccessible. For another, in the tradition of Prohibition, the marijuana industry was a major source of money for some of the towns in the surrounding counties. No county official looked too hard in the rugged areas—the local economy was dependent to a startling degree on the drug dollars. Moreover, the "drug wars" provided a convenient explanation for the occasional bodies that were found. Solving those killings was not a priority item.

In retrospect Lyons also realized something else. It had to do with Brognola's willingness to go to Plan Two. In order to get the Justice Department to play along, the orders must have come from somebody high up.

Very high up. Maybe as high up as you can go in this country.

As usual, he thought sourly, the poor schmuck on the front line never knows about the games behind the games. But maybe it has to be that way. "Orders is orders," and all that.

At least now they had their orders, to the max—Brognola's last words to Lyons had been clear on that point.

"Oh, and Ironman?"

"Yes, boss."

"Don't come back unless Krasne's out of the picture. Permanently."

"Ten-four."

Now they were in Ukiah, in the heart of California's lush forest and wine country, catching an early breakfast at the Country Kitchen Restaurant.

The food arrived and they dug in.

"Don't you ever worry about cholesterol?" Chandler inquired as Lyons forked down rare steak swabbed in egg yolk.

Lyons winked. He was feeling fine. They had the target, and they had the green light to go after it. Their way.

"I don't worry about a lot of problems that might crop up in my senior-citizen years. Social security. The national debt. Whether the world will be hopelessly polluted. It's like a reverse gamble. If I live that long, *then* I'll worry about my arteries and all that other stuff. If I don't, who cares?''

Ukiah fell behind them as Lyons drove the van up Highway 101. They drove past miles of vineyards and several wineries before Lyons left 101 and headed east on a two-lane paved road that plunged into the forests.

Two hours later they could have been in a different country.

It was wilderness all the way. The road rose and fell in the foothills. Towering conifers pressed in on the road, which was flanked at ground level by tangled green undergrowth.

Though it was midmorning, the northern California fog blanketed the highway. By noon it would be gone, but for now it struggled against the June sun. The battle was nip and tuck. Fog lay in dense patches in some areas, followed by stretches of sunlight in others.

''Are we in Indian country yet?'' inquired Blancanales. The term was a holdover from his Vietnam days.

Gadgets was poring over a topographic map. ''Affirmative. But as far as we know, it's cool. They shouldn't have any idea we're here.''

They entered a patch of particularly heavy fog, real pea-soup stuff that forced Lyons to slow to a crawl. He turned on the van's headlights.

Another set of headlights suddenly showed behind them. They made fuzzy yellow circles in the light-diffusing fog. The height of the headlights said the vehicle had to be a large pickup or something comparable. It pulled up close behind them.

''Slow down, you idiot,'' muttered Lyons, his eyes on the rear-view mirror.

''Tailgater?'' asked Blancanales.

''Yeah. Some jerk that doesn't realize you don't go sixty on a mountain road in the fog. I'm going to let him by.''

"Any chance he's a hostile?" inquired Chandler.

"Negative. Probably some mountain man dope grower, or maybe a tourist who got lost." He pulled closer to the right shoulder.

A sound like a jackhammer punching against the van's chassis shattered the foggy stillness.

"On second thought, make that affirmative!"

20

"Indian country!" shouted Chandler.

The warning was unnecessary. The men of Able Team scrambled for their guns.

Lyons slammed on the brakes. Tires screeched as the front of the van nosed downward in a skid. Their pursuers shot by them on the left.

It was a pickup truck, a big four-by-four. Two men knelt in the bed, aiming automatic weapons at them. Tongues of orange flame licked out from the fog.

Blancanales, who was riding shotgun, swiveled in his bucket seat and raised an M-16. "Go around them on the left!" he shouted.

Lyons punched the accelerator. Rubber smoked as the van leaped forward. The men in the back of the four-by turned toward them as Lyons shot by. The flames licked out again, followed by the clanging of 9 mm hits to the van.

It was drowned out by Blancanales's auto-burn reply.

The former Green Beret half knelt, half crouched on the bucket seat. He had the M-16 clamped against his side, spraying a hail of three thousand feet-per-second projectiles at the attackers—and spraying a hail of hot brass into the interior of the van.

Lyons raised his right shoulder and elbow in a protective shrug, turning his face partly to the left to avoid the stream of empty cartridge cases. The brass bounced off the men and pinged against the walls of the van as the clip-fed rounds blazed through the rifle.

"Jesus, Pol! I hope they're taking as many hits as we are!" Lyons yelled as he fought to control the van.

They were.

The first burst center-punched the windshield directly in front of the driver. The high-velocity slugs smashed a hole the size of a saucer in the safety glass. However, due to the concentration of the bullets' energy, it didn't even crack the rest of the window.

They also smashed a hole the size of a saucer in the driver's chest.

His body bounced backward against the seat back. The angle jammed the dead man's foot against the accelerator and the four-by-four leaped forward. At the same time, Lyons braked sharply, allowing the truck to zoom up to be even with them again.

The combined effects of the four-by's acceleration and Lyons's braking were so sudden that the gunman nearest the cab actually escaped Pol's deadly fire.

For a moment, anyway.

Blancanales's second burst caught the other gunman in the head. His skull exploded into a mist of red droplets and brain. His body, instantly limp, subsided onto the sidewall of the pickup, his shoulders and the bloody remains of his head over the edge. A stream of red poured down the outside of the truck. The rush of the passing air spread it into a fan-shaped stream of crimson rivulets down the outside of the truck bed.

The Politician instantly refocused his attention on the first gunman, the one nearest the front. He was in a semi-crouch, struggling to regain his balance from the lurching of the truck.

He never made it. Blancanales swung the muzzle of the M-16 into line, and a burst of .223 slugs tore into the attacker's body. The impact lifted him to his feet and staggered him backward. Either the wind stream over the cab or another burst from Pol—maybe it was both—flipped him out the far side of the bed onto the foggy pavement.

With nothing but dead men in it, the four-by careered off to the right, hit the shoulder, skidded and rolled.

The Able Team van skidded to a stop.

"More coming, Ironman," advised Blancanales calmly. He had heard brakes screech, followed by the solid thump of a body hitting a chassis moments after the gunman's body flipped out of the truck.

Moments later another vehicle loomed out of the fog behind them.

Lyons caught a glimpse of a dirt road leading off into the forest, barely visible in the mist. He jerked the wheel and stomped on the gas pedal. With a roar of power and a screech of tires, the van leaped down the road.

Blancanales twisted the nearly empty clip from his rifle and slammed another into place.

Gadgets, meanwhile, had busied himself by unzipping a nylon gun case and removing the weapon inside. In the relative silence when the bullets and brass momentarily stopped flying, Chandler glanced at the weapon.

He remembered it from the first time he had seen Able Team fight. He'd never seen one before or since.

It looked like a conventional riot shotgun had gotten together for an all-American quickie with an M-16, and this was the offspring. A drum magazine suggested maybe they'd made it a *ménage à trois*, with the third participant being an old Thompson submachine gun.

Gadgets followed his gaze and grinned. "Shotgun," he said simply.

Blancanales glanced back and winked, "Sporter, is all. He uses it for dove and quail."

"Right," agreed Chandler facetiously.

The weapon was the Konzak assault shotgun. Twelve gauge, it could be fired either as a full automatic or a semi-auto, or, as Lyons liked to put it, halfway in between.

"Meaning?" Chandler had asked.

"Meaning full-auto, but three-shot bursts. SEALs used them in Vietnam. Hell of a weapon."

The twenty-round drum would be loaded, Mike knew, with rifled slugs alternated every other round with double-ought buck.

The Konzak took no prisoners.

Gadgets unzipped another case and pulled out an M-16 that he handed to Chandler. "Here, Counselor."

"Thanks." As Mike accepted the weapon, a wave of something akin to nostalgia washed over him.

The M-16. Vietnam workhorse. Chandler hefted it, felt the configuration and weight, saw the dull, drab, unglamorous finish. The brown metal of the van's interior faded, and he saw instead dense jungle, gently moving elephant grass, and the pesky wait-a-minute vines.

Nam. He'd been there. He'd done it. And it was there that he had met Mack Bolan. It was there that he had learned the true lessons of life.

The gut-tingling thrill of laying it all on the line for the simple reason that it felt right to do it, never mind getting your ass shot off, and never mind what Hanoi Jane and the draft dodgers sang about.

The strangely detached feeling as you checked the enemy dead and then your own, knowing that one of the shattered bodies could be you the next time.

And the strange, indefinable feeling of superiority when you knew you were better than the rest because you did the hard stuff simply because you *could* do it, not because you *had* to.

If the peacetime civilian prosecutor in him had already been in critical condition, it gave up the ghost and died now. Rest in peace.

Blancanales's voice drew him back to reality.

"Here they come, guys."

Carl Lyons spoke over his shoulder as he maneuvered the van over the rough dirt tracks.

"How many?"

His voice showed no tension. Blancanales, still turned around in the passenger seat, studied the fog behind them.

"Looks like two—no, make that three, four vehicles."

"Describe!"

"Looks like a camper, a blue van, another camper and..." He suddenly laughed.

"And what?"

"So help me, God, it looks like an old Impala, yellow, or maybe its a Bonneville. Sixties era."

"Any four-wheelers?"

"Negative."

"Distance?"

"Thirty yards."

The van crashed down on its undercarriage as the path dipped sharply into the bottom of a dry streambed. Lyons fought the wheel and gunned up the other side. From the back of the van, Gadgets spoke up.

"Any ideas, Ironman?"

"Yeah. Hope for a clear space in the fog, so we can put some distance between them and us."

"That's nice. Anything else?"

"Yep. We gotta surround 'em."

Even as he spoke, the fog seemed to lift. Lyons floored the accelerator. The engine roared and gravel flew as the van urged ahead. The gap between pursued and pursuers widened as Able Team took advantage of the increased visibility while the enemy was still in the fog bank.

"Perfect!" exclaimed Lyons.

Chandler, however, had been considering Lyons's plan. He'd spent his recent months pushing law books, and it was taking him a while to get up to battle speed.

"You said 'we gotta surround 'em?'" he asked slowly.

"Right."

Chandler nodded thoughtfully. The silence was broken only by the growl of the van's engine and the squeak of the body as it twisted and dipped on the rough road. Finally the prosecutor spoke again.

"If you don't mind my asking," he began.

"No, go right ahead," said Lyons agreeably.

"There's at least four of them. Four vehicles, that is. Right?"

"Correct."

"And one of us, one vehicle."

"True enough," Lyons agreed.

Chandler thought it over. No matter how he looked at it, the result was the same. "And we are gonna surround them?" he asked finally.

"Right. And ambush 'em." The Ironman grinned, enjoying Chandler's discomfort.

Behind Mike's back, Gadgets winked at Blancanales. They began preparing for the ambush with a practiced efficiency. They had been there before.

First came the M-16/M-203, the hybrid assault rifle/grenade launcher, hardly a new weapon these days but a workhorse of death by firepower. Gadgets laid three of them out, side by side, on the cluttered center floor.

Added to each pile were .45 automatic pistols, honed and balanced.

Nylon pouches, o.d. in color, containing 40 mm steel wire fragmentation grenades came next. Mike could remember the exploding, slicing carnage they could inflict.

Bandoleers containing magazines of ammunition for the assault rifles came next. Finally, Gadgets produced Kevlar and steel body armor, a hybrid between the latest lightweight bulletproof vests of synthetic nylon derivatives and the heavy armor plating of knights of old. The combination would stop most conventional handgun ammo, leaving the wearer only sore, bruised, perhaps with the wind knocked out of him—which, as Lyons had once remarked, was a hell of a lot better than being blown to pieces.

Nobody had disputed the wisdom of his words.

The van swayed and bumped then forged ahead like a relentless ship. The clock was ticking downward toward showdown.

21

"Let's do it here!"

Lyons punched the accelerator. The van surged to a rise then skidded to a locked-wheel stop at the top. Blancanales bailed out, M-16 in hand, and sprinted up ahead. His eyes strained to penetrate the pea-soup fog that once again enveloped them.

The terrain was flat for a distance of maybe fifteen feet at the crest of the rise where the van now waited. Beyond that, it sloped down again. The slope rapidly increased in pitch, so that ten or fifteen yards farther it was approaching drop-off proportions.

We've got no choice but to do it here, Blancanales thought.

It was the end of the line. The trail had petered out.

As nearly as he could make out in the mist, the drop-off was about fifteen or twenty feet into a draw that ran off to the right.

"Perfect!" the Politician said aloud. He turned and sprinted back to the van. In the distance, engines strained as the attackers closed the gap.

Next, Blancanales checked the terrain behind the van. An outcropping of rock the size of a house jutted up to the left of the path. A jumble of smaller boulders flanked the path to the right.

Not perfect, but pretty good.

"Well?" Lyons inquired.

"It starts to drop off pretty steeply up ahead twenty yards or so," Blancanales reported.

"Enough to trap 'em?"

"That's affirmative."

Lyons didn't hesitate. He jammed the van into gear and drove forward, leaving Blancanales standing at the top of the rise.

He almost overdid it. By the time he had braked, then thrown it into reverse, the van was at the point of no return. For a heart-stopping moment they struggled against the pull of gravity, fighting the drop-off into the canyon. Then the spinning rear wheels caught hold, and the van roared back up to the rise where Pol stood.

"Hard left!" The former Green Beret waved them over, and Lyons drove behind the houselike outcropping, then killed the engine. Behind them the roar of engines grew louder.

Lyons, Gadgets and Chandler bailed out of the van without hesitation. Blancanales hastily erased the tire tracks to the outcropping where the van now waited.

"The oldest trick in the book," said Chandler, shaking his head.

"And still effective," rejoined Gadgets.

"You hope."

"*We* hope, you mean."

The four men hastily buckled on the body armor. Then they draped on the other gear Gadgets had laid out.

Blancanales finished his task of obliterating the tracks and turned to Lyons. "Almost go over the cliff, Ironman?" he asked with a grin.

"Remind me to show you what twenty yards is," grumbled Lyons, shouldering a pouch of grenades.

"Twenty yards, fifteen yards, twenty-five yards. What's the difference in the grand scheme of things?"

"There's a hell of a difference when there's a cliff at sixteen yards."

"Details. I'm a lover, not a fighter."

"Yeah, right." The roar of engines told them the time for jiving was over. Lyons turned to Chandler. "You stick with me. We'll go up here to the left." He gestured to the outcropping that concealed the van. "Pol, you and Gadgets take cover in those rocks to the right of the trail."

"Ten-four."

"If they go for it, hopefully at least one or two will go over the drop-off. If we're real lucky, they all will. Then it's just a question of moving up and shooting fish in a barrel. Otherwise, we'll take out the guys who don't go over, then move up and do the rest."

The men nodded. Gadgets shouldered the M-16/M-203 over one arm and slung a pouch of grenades over the other. Blancanales did likewise.

Lyons took the Konzak.

"Question," said Chandler.

"Shoot."

"What happens if they don't go for it and stop at the top of the rise?"

Lyons gave a thin smile. "Then the chances are I won't have to worry about all that cholesterol. Let's move it."

FOR A MOMENT, it looked as if Mike's fears would be realized. The lead vehicle was a camper on a half-ton truck. It crested the top and slowed so suddenly it slid sideways for a few feet.

Go on, you assholes, we're down there, Chandler urged mentally, as if to will them to proceed.

"Come on, boys, keep going," Lyons said quietly.

Nothing happened. The driver scanned the road ahead, cocking his head as if to listen. Then abruptly he surged ahead, down the dwindling path, following the tracks of Lyons's van.

Jackpot! thought Mike.

He shot a glance at Lyons. The rugged blond soldier winked. Then, to the prosecutor's bewilderment, he thought he heard humming.

He strained to hear. Yes, there it was.

> Dum, da-dum dum;
> Dum, da-dum dum;
> Dum, dum, dum, dum dum!

Chandler tried to place the tune, but it eluded him. For some reason, though, he thought of high school and the football team. Then he had it—the universal "fight song," that had its origins who knows where. Mike's high school had been named Lincoln, which didn't fit the beat, so their version had been more general.

> On to vic—t'ry,
> On to vic—t'ry,
> Fight and win this game!

Lyons was humming the alma mater fight song on the brink of a firefight!

Chandler crouched behind the rock and watched. The other camper and the blue van followed in close order. The yellow Bonneville wallowed along some thirty yards behind, wheels spinning as it struggled up the rise.

The timing was perfect.

The driver of the lead pickup saw the drop-off. Maybe he saw the reversal of Lyons's tracks, as well. But if he did, it came too late to do any good.

He jammed his foot onto the brake, standing on it. The wheels locked up, but the only effect was to put him into a skid as they went off over the edge.

The van and the second pickup fared better. Their drivers saw what happened ahead in time to slide to a stop right on the brink.

Behind them, and now up above them, Able Team heard the crash of the first pickup. So did the driver of the Bonneville, and he slid the car to a stop on the crest of the rise.

Lyons and Chandler could see the large sedan had several people inside. The dark oulines of weapons were visible inside the car.

"Come on, boys, come to papa," breathed Lyons.

As if they heard him, four men bailed out of the old Pontiac. They were maybe forty feet from Lyons and Chandler. The main problem was to avoid having Gadgets and Blancanales in the field of fire.

Not to worry. The two veteran Able Team members flattened out behind the rocks.

"Now!" commanded Lyons.

This time there was no announcement of intent to arrest. It was shoot first, ask questions later.

As luck would have it, Chandler and Lyons both fired at the same man first. Simultaneous bursts from the M-16 and the Konzak caught the man in the torso. The loads made an audible *whump!* as they hit. A fine spray of blood flew into the air as the biker's body was hurled up into the air and backward against the hood of the car. He lay sprawled across the windshield, and a river of blood ran down the yellow metal of the hood.

Then Lyons and Chandler got in sync.

The prosecutor swung left and took out the man in that direction. Lyons swung right and eliminated the other two like he was painting over graffiti with a massive spray gun.

Chandler's burst caught his target in the shoulder area. It knocked him against the car. Mike fired again and missed, the bullets peppering the metal of the car door with a sharp metallic clank. He corrected his aim and slowed the rate of fire, deliberately placing three very short bursts of three or four each into the twitching body as the man staggered and leaned against the car.

Lyons had no such trouble. The slugs and buckshot from the Konzak slammed one man into the other in a ghastly embrace of death. Then he poured two more bursts into the two figures.

"Let's go!" Lyons snapped. The Able Team leader was off and running, even before the two bodies had slumped to the ground. Below the Bonneville, Gadgets and Blancanales moved forward, as well.

Chandler ran after Lyons, keeping low and using the boulders for concealment. Crazily, he found himself humming the fight song, "dum, da-dum, dum; dum, da-dum, dum; dum, dum, dum, dum, dum."

"Heads!"

Lyons shouted the warning as he and Blancanales arched grenades at the two vehicles below them. A moment later a third grenade appeared, this one flying higher and farther. It went over the drop-off to the camper below.

Twin blasts shook the ground.

Chandler was vaguely aware of a detached arm flying out from among the rest of the unrecognizable meat. A leg went in the other direction. A part of Mike's mind wondered morbidly if they had belonged to the same person.

"Don't mess with us, you bastards. It'll cost you an arm and a leg."

Somebody down there was still alive and moving. A spray of slugs hit a boulder in front of Lyons, spattering him with lead fragments and bits of granite.

Able Team returned fire.

Lyons was on the far left. Chandler was fifteen or so feet to his right, near the center of the arc. Still farther to the right, across the path and down a ways, were Blancanales and Gadgets.

It made a deadly semicircle of fire.

The Konzak and the M-16s hammered relentlessly at the would-be killers. Two of them leaped downhill, away from the lethal firestorm. The rest died where they were.

Suddenly a burst of fire came from the far right. It sprayed screaming projectiles and chips of rock over Able Team. There were at least three men, who had come up from below them.

Able Team ducked and flattened against the ground, squeezing every centimeter of concealment from the rocks. Then Gadgets, who was on the edge of a draw, suddenly gave a spasmodic jerk and slid out of sight into the gully.

His M-16/M-203 stayed where he had been.

Oh, no! thought Chandler as he hugged the ground beneath the insane streaks of death above him. Lyons twisted his body to reach for a grenade from the pouch.

Suddenly there was a new sound. It was a hollow booming. It came from the gully where Gadgets had disappeared.

One of the attackers who was pinning them down did a sudden back flip, his body swatted into the air as though by a giant baseball bat. Almost instantly a second one did the same thing.

The Konzak! thought Chandler. He'd forgotten that along with the M-16 Gadgets had taken one slung over his shoulder.

There was one more man in that direction. Whatever else he was, he was not a coward.

Undaunted by the sudden violent disappearance of his comrades, he swung an Uzi to face Gadgets and the assault shotgun. But the fire that had pinned the rest of Able Team and Chandler was gone, and Pol reacted instantly, swinging the M-16 to bear on the man.

Both bursts hit simultaneously. Together they made the old and the new of kill-power and ballistics. The M-16 poured supersonic light-weight projectiles into the man's body, while the Konzak hurled slow, heavy, lumbering chunks of lead.

The killer's body splattered across the rocky landscape.

Suddenly there was silence. As suddenly as it had begun, it was over.

As the ringing in their ears subsided, another sound replaced it. Drip-drip-drip-drip-drip, on and on, like a leaky faucet, as blood flowed to the fingertips of a dead biker draped over the hood of one of the campers. The blood spattered onto a flat rock below his body.

They waited and listened, ears straining in the foggy morning air.

Nothing moved. The drips slowed, became less frequent, then died out altogether.

Finally Lyons got to his feet.

Gadgets was clambering up the bank. Blood soaked his shoulder, but he waved away any questions with a terse "Just a nick."

Lyons scanned the area for signs of life. He cocked his head to listen some more then nodded to the others to get up.

"Like I said, we'll surround 'em."

Chandler nodded, his heart pounding from the adrenaline that had been pumped into his body. "One thing, though," he observed.

Lyons looked at him. "What's that?"

"We forgot to arrest 'em."

22

Despite Lyons's seemingly lighthearted comment, they inspected the bodies without speaking.

In all, thirteen dead. No survivors.

As the battle adrenaline wore off, the wilderness silence somehow seemed even more acute. All of them felt it. No matter how much killing a man did, there was always an emotional emptiness when the fight was over. Always, that is, unless the guy was one of the twisted ones who enjoyed making people dead, for reasons that weren't entirely wholesome.

Every death scene had a "feel" to it.

It was as though the emotional energy—the vibes—that existed at the time of death somehow lingered afterward, permeating the site.

Sometimes the feel was one of anger, as though the death resulted from a vicious fight on both sides. These were the "hot blood" killings.

Sometimes the feel was one of squalor and desperation, the ghetto killings that exploded when the poverty and heat and crowding went beyond the limits of the killer's tolerance.

In other cases the feel was one of queasy sickness. It was usually present when the killing was done by a psychopath, particularly where there were sexual overtones to it. Some-

:imes vibès of great pain seemed to be present, in the tor-
:ure/murders, for instance.

Early in his career as a patrol cop, Lyons had learned to
respect these sensations. In those days he was often the first
on the scene of a homicide. And, though it was nothing he
could ever testify to in court, these feelings often furnished
a subconscious background that shaped the investigation.

They were almost invariably right on the money.

Chandler had experienced the same thing. He had made
it a habit to visit the scene of every homicide case he prosecuted. Moreover, he tried to do it at the same time of day as
the killing had likely occurred, even if that happened to be
two o'clock in the morning.

Other D.A.'s said he was crazy.

He had passed it off on the pretext of checking out the
distances, lighting, the location of things, so he could better understand the testimony of the witnesses. And that was
all true.

But what he didn't say was that, like Lyons, he firmly believed he could soak up the vibes, even weeks or months
later. Yet that was the truth.

Now, as they checked the bodies, there was a curious lack
of a definable feel to this death scene. Maybe it was because this was more professional, more like a war. The
combatants didn't know each other and were essentially
faceless.

The struggle would therefore be somehow more detached. The emotions present would be only the normal
ones of excitement and fear and pain. There wouldn't be
some identifiable, overriding theme such as anger, jeal-
ousy, or psychological sickness.

Chandler found that lack of a dominant emotion to be
disquieting in itself.

Maybe it was because he'd been away from the soldier business for too long. Maybe he'd fallen prey to the liberal's misconception that there has to be a reason to kill somebody, an emotional reason. Maybe he just didn't want to accept what he knew to be true—that some people would kill other people just because they were in the way.

Or just for the hell of it.

Yet that's what it was all about. That's why Able Team and Stony Man and, ultimately, Mack Bolan, were there in the first place.

The equalizers. The balancers of the books. The eveners of the score.

Somebody had to do it. If the courts didn't want the responsibility of justice, he knew somebody who did.

"No Crank," Lyons announced when they completed the inspection.

Blancanales nodded. "So we noticed."

"How many more guys like this do you suppose he's got?" mused the Ironman.

Blancanales shrugged. "No way of telling. One thing for sure, though. These guys weren't the best we've ever gone up against, but they weren't total rookies, either. They've gotten some training from somewhere."

"It stands to reason," continued Lyons, "that Krasne and the rest of his men are at the main facility. They'll be waiting for a report, and they will have heard this little firefight."

"No element of surprise," agreed Gadgets. "They knew we were coming. That's something we'll have to look into someday. Meantime, what's the plan?"

Lyons grimaced. "Surround 'em and attack, I guess. Unless somebody's got a better idea."

Nobody did.

Twenty minutes later, Lyons pulled the van to the side of the road and stopped.

"I make it we're within a mile."

Gadgets and Chandler were examining the topo map. "That's about right," the prosecutor reported.

They had retraced their route back to the main road. Then in another two miles or so, they found the access road to Crank's property.

They took that slowly, both to keep the engine noise down and to check for lookouts.

Lyons found a suitable place and drove the van off into the woods. Thirty feet, and the vehicle was all but invisible from the road. He killed the engine.

The sun was burning through the fog as they loaded on their gear. They removed the tracks of the van as much as possible, kicking the weeds and undergrowth back to something approximating the way they had been before the tires flattened them. Then they set off on foot.

As the girl with the "Red's #1 Old Lady" shirt had said, the country was beautiful. The footing was good. The terrain wasn't particularly tough, at least not compared to some of the mountains and jungles Able Team had hiked. They were there in less than twenty minutes.

Lying prone, they scanned the scene with field glasses.

An irregular clearing had been cut into the forest. Lyons estimated it at two or three acres, plus a dirt runway that angled off from the far side. A light plane, a Beechcraft, was tied down at the near end of the landing strip.

A large, L-shaped ranch house dominated the clearing. Beyond it were two older log cabins and an ugly square concrete-block structure. A single marijuana plant, sensemilla, Lyons noted, grew near the house.

The main crop would be somewhere else, he thought. This must be just somebody's pet plant.

"Surround 'em and attack?" whispered Gadgets at last.

Lyons started to speak. He was cut short by the sudden chop-chop-chop of an approaching helicopter. The men twisted and looked overhead.

A Bell Huey was coming at them in a diving swoop. They didn't bother to wonder where Krasne had gotten his hands on one.

"Scatter!" shouted Lyons.

They did, sprinting in separate directions like the corners of an expanding square.

Lyons dove over a fallen log and wedged himself against it. Blancanales, master of cover and concealment that he was, spotted a crevice in the rocky ground. It looked as though it wouldn't conceal a child, but when he flattened into it, he was all but invisible.

Gadgets sprinted for a clump of rocks and dived over them as machine-gun bullets kicked up a line of dots and dashes after him. He sailed into the air, intending to hug up to whatever cover the rocks would provide.

Only there wasn't any. The rocks were on the edge of a rise that sloped off steeply, though not vertically, on the other side.

"Shit!"

The word showed both amazement and a little amusement. He sailed into space, "swimming" with his hands so as not to rotate heels over head and land skull first when he finally hit. It was about a fifteen-foot drop, though at the time it looked like fifty.

He landed heavily on his right shoulder. At least there were no rocks, and the downhill slope provided some distance for his body to absorb the impact. It helped, but not enough. He felt the shoulder separate as he hit.

Mike Chandler ran like a man possessed. Then he realized he wouldn't make it.

The cover he had been going for was too far. The chopping roar of the helicopter sounded right behind him, gaining fast.

To hell with it. When there's nothing else left, attack. Slim is better than none, where chances are concerned. And if you eat it, maybe you'll at least help out the other guys.

He skidded to a halt and turned. The M-16 was on autoburn. He clamped the stock into his side, under his right upper arm. Left hand on the fore stock, he swiveled around and up, clamping down on the trigger as he did so.

His face contorted with battle rage as the weapon bucked in his hands.

He held the trigger down and he kept it there.

For a moment there was only the thunder of the guns, Chandler's and the helicopter's. A line of dusty impacts zipped up the slope towards the lone warrior. Then suddenly the diving chopper seemed to come apart as Chandler's sustained auto-burn came on to target.

A ball of bright orange flame roiled upward. The heavy *whoop!* of the explosion filled the air. Then the petrochemical fireball dissolved into thick black smoke, and pieces of the chopper continued to fall to the ground for what seemed to Lyons and the others like a long time.

They fell around Gadgets as he lay clutching his shoulder on the slope.

They fell around Blancanales, wedged in the crack in the earth's surface.

They fell on the fallen log where Lyons had taken cover.

And they fell on the body of Mike Chandler.

The prosecutor lay on his back. His left hand lay near his side. His right arm was flung over his head, hand still clamped around the pistol grip of the now empty M-16.

A single round hole, half an inch in diameter, was centered where the upturned neck joined the chest.

His eyes stared upward, where the chopper would have passed if he hadn't been what he was.

A warrior. A man.

23

Three men took the house.

They strapped the gun stock to an M-16 tight against Gadgets's right side then clamped his upper arm against it. He fit his right hand around the pistol grip of the M-16 and held it tightly. More binding went around the outside, immobilizing the damaged shoulder and holding the weapon in place.

"Tighter."

Blancanales tested the bandages. "It's tight enough."

"Tighter!" Gadgets's face was grim, angry.

The Politician shrugged and did as he was asked.

Gadgets tried it out. The weapon was effectively clamped to his body. His right hand reached to the pistol grip and trigger. The wrappings were tight enough that he could probably even operate the weapon one-handed, for short bursts, anyway. But that wouldn't be necessary, because his good left arm was available to steady the weapon, to replace clips, or do whatever was needed.

"Feel okay?"

Gadgets didn't tell them that it hurt like hell. Feeling the pain was at the same time a monument and a duty to those who had fallen. If you can hurt, you're alive. There were a hell of a lot of dead folks who would probably jump at the chance to feel that pain.

Jaw set, he savored the sensation.

"All set," he announced at last.

Able Team formed a grim fire team and advanced in textbook fashion. Covering fire from two, while one sprinted for the next piece of concealment. Then covering fire from him and one of the others, while the third did ditto.

In a matter of minutes they had leapfrogged up to the main house.

There were no legal formalities at the door.

Borrowing from their experience at Red's house, Able Team made it look like the front door was their main target, when in fact it was the window. Blancanales autoburned from the M-16 at the door. Simultaneously Lyons popped up at the window and hosed down the interior with thundering sweeps from the gun.

Clips were dumped and replaced, and the team was inside.

Nothing moved. Blood had spattered the walls from Lyons's volley.

"Krasne!" Lyons bellowed the word.

A scraggly haired biker popped into view from the hall. Slugs from two M-16s hit him immediately, longer bursts than they had to be.

A fusillade of shots burst from the first room down the hall.

Lyons's M-16 jammed, and he dropped it with a curse and drew the .45. Able Team returned the fire, ten for one.

Suddenly there was a sound from the room at the end of the long hall. It was the muffled shriek of a woman, cut short by the meaty smack of open hand against flesh.

"Krasne!" Lyons yelled again.

"Die, pigs!" Krasne's shape suddenly appeared in the doorway, a Mac 10 in his hand. The weapon chattered. Deadly 9 mm slugs peppered the room.

As Able Team dived for cover, Krasne's attention was distracted by something behind him. Glass broke as the girl slugged him with a quart-size beer bottle. Then she broke past him and started to run down the hall.

"Help me!" she sobbed. "Kill him!"

Lyons started forward, but Krasne was too quick. He snatched at the girl's upper arm and whipped her back to him. Then his arm was around her waist, and he was clutching her to him, using her as a shield.

She was dead.

Ballistically speaking, she was a goner if Blancanales decided to shoot. With the M-16 either one of them could shoot right through the girl and nail Krasne.

For some reason neither did, even though it was the logical thing to do.

Strangely, Lyons didn't mind. It had become somehow important to try to save one life in this house of death.

"Kill him!" the girl screamed.

Everything seemed to happen in dreadful slow motion.

She lifted her feet off the ground, forcing him to support her whole weight. At the same time she leaned forward, bending her body around Krasne's massive forearm.

The massive outlaw biker no longer had a shield.

The sudden shift in weight pulled him forward, off balance. The girl struggled to curl herself around his arm.

"You bitch!" The words exploded in a guttural snarl. Krasne's features were distorted with hatred.

"Kill him!" she shrieked again. "Do it, do it, do it!"

They did it.

Lyons's arm moved up from his side. It made a sweeping arc with the .45 Government Model in his hand.

It didn't slow down when it came into line. There was no aiming. No cop-approved two-fisted grip. Just a single snap shot as the weapon swept up.

One Silvertip slug. Four hundred foot-pounds of energy slamming into Krasne's chest.

The point of impact was a few inches to the right of center, and a couple of inches below the collarbone. The sledgehammer blow rocked him back. His left arm jerked, and the girl fell free. She landed in a heap at his feet, sobbing hysterically.

A muscle spasm in Crank's right arm caused the Mac 10 to fire twice.

The shots were full-auto, but aimless. The sound was almost a single report, with only a slight stutter between the two explosions. The slugs went off at a downward and sideways angle. Sparks flew from the cement floor and ricochets whined off in the distance.

"Catch, Ironman!"

It was all-pro, all the way.

With his good arm, Gadgets palmed a fresh clip of ammo from somewhere and flipped it to Lyons. The Ironman plucked it out of the air with his left hand at the same time that his right thumb hit the magazine release button on the .45. As the empty clip fell clear of the gun, Lyons clapped the fresh one in and hit the slide release.

The slide slammed forward at the same time as the empty magazine clinked on the concrete floor.

Quick as it was, it wasn't quick enough.

Even as the clip arced toward Lyons, Krasne took a quick half step forward and recovered his balance. The Mac 10 steadied in his right hand, and he was in control again.

The autoweapon came around. The same guttural snarl of rage tore from his throat.

"You fucker!"

The Mac 10 steadied on its target even as the slide rammed shut on Lyons's .45. Then Krasne's weapon was chattering its 9 mm death.

The girl on the ground gave a single short bark as the first slug hit her back. Her body twitched and jerked as the bullets hit.

Lyons's .45 boomed three times. The 9 mm autofire was chopped short.

Krasne stumbled backward and went down. The Mac 10 fell from his hand.

The Ironman walked over to the fallen outlaw biker. He walked slowly, almost stiffly, as if he were supremely weary. Then he was standing over the man, gazing down, his mind working with a curious, emotionless detachment.

Danny Williams and his partner.

Hogan, whose final wink would stay with Lyons forever.

The guards on the armored truck.

The other Strike Force members who died on the search warrant episode.

Red's #1 Old Lady, killed as they questioned her.

Now this girl, blown to pieces as she lay at his feet.

Most of all, Mike Chandler, who had taken a slug to the neck while he brought down the chopper from Crank's little army.

The tab came to one hell of a high figure. Krasne's account was overdrawn. No more credit. Time to close the books.

"Crank!" Lyons barked it like an order.

The biker moved slightly where he lay on the floor. His head turned. The eyes, wide and shocked, suddenly narrowed into focus. They gazed balefully at Lyons.

"Crank, look at me!"

The Able Team leader raised the .45. It boomed one last time. The massive body spasmed, and then the eyes weren't focused any longer.

Lyons let the gun down to his side. When he spoke, his voice was soft, almost sad.

"You're under arrest, fucker."

EPILOGUE

"How much?" Lyons took out his wallet.

The clerk consulted the cash register tape and announced the figure. He was a lanky youth with a pale complexion that contrasted sharply with his dark hair.

Lyons counted out the bills and handed them to him.

"It's not assembled, you know," the clerk said.

Lyons nodded. "I was wondering if you would do that for me?"

The clerk shook his head. "Sorry. All we do is sell 'em. It's up to you to put it together."

"All right." The Ironman shrugged. He picked up the bulky carton and maneuvered it out the door and to his car. That night he and Margie put it together in the living room of her La Crescenta condominium.

Then the damn thing didn't want to fit in the rental car, but he finally managed it.

The next morning, bright and early, he was ready.

He drove to the intersection a couple of blocks away from where Red's house had been. Easing the car to the curb, he killed the engine and waited.

The early-summer haze hung over the area as it had what seemed a lifetime ago when they had done the search warrants. The day Hogan died with a wink and a leap.

He felt painfully alone as the names and faces of the ones who were gone scrolled before him.

Then he heard it.

A battered station wagon turned the corner. The driver was a woman. From what Lyons could see, the woman's family was poor. They were also good people.

The car slowed and the kid got out, paper in hand. He dashed up to the sidewalk and pitched the folded missile. It landed right on the doorstep.

It was the same kid. A good paperboy. None of your front-lawn action.

As the boy trotted back to his mother's car, Lyons got out of his rental and walked over. They both saw him, a rugged blond man with tired eyes, and were instantly wary. Lyons reached for the Justice Department badge he had borrowed so they wouldn't be afraid.

Anybody watching would have seen them talk for a few minutes then the man and boy walk to the man's car.

Where they unloaded the new bicycle.

The heavy-duty deluxe paperboy model.

Bright red.

JACK ADRIAN

DEATH LANDS

**When all is lost,
there's always the future.**

The world blew out in 2001.

On a crisp clear January day, a presidential inauguration day, a one-megaton blast ripped through the Soviet embassy in Washington, D.C., power base of the United States and political center of the Western world.

Simultaneous explosions around the globe changed the face and shape of the earth forever. Out of the ruins emerges Deathlands, a world that conspires against survival.

In this hostile environment of strontium swamps and nuclear night, Ryan Cawdor, a survivalist and warrior, teams up with the beautiful Krysty Wroth and armorer J. B. Dix in an adventure to unlock the secrets of the pre-war scientific experiments that may hold the answer to survival in the Deathlands of the future.

4 FREE BOOKS
1 FREE GIFT
NO RISK
NO OBLIGATION
NO KIDDING
